GW00393455

The Old School

The Old School

A study in the Oddities
of the English Public School System

SIMON RAVEN

HAMISH HAMILTON
LONDON

First published in Great Britain 1986
by Hamish Hamilton Ltd
27 Wrights Lane, London w8 5TZ

Copyright © 1986 by Simon Raven

Two verses from 'Three Odes of Horace' translated
by Louis MacNeice, which appear on page 28 are
reprinted by permission of Faber and Faber Ltd,
from *The Collected Poems of Louis MacNeice*

British Library Cataloguing in Publication Data

Raven, Simon
    The old school: a study in the oddities of
    the English public school system.
    1. Public schools, Endowed (Great Britain)
    I. Title
    373.18'092'4   LA635
    ISBN 0-241-11929-4

Typeset by Rowland Phototypesetting Ltd, Bury St Edmunds, Suffolk
Printed in Great Britain by
St Edmundsbury Press Ltd, Bury St Edmunds, Suffolk

List of Illustrations

Cricket on the Head at Tonbridge (reproduced by permission of the BBC Hulton Picture Library)

Football at Rugby (reproduced by permission of the BBC Hulton Picture Library)

First Love. Illustration from *Tom Brown's Schooldays* (reproduced by permission of the Mary Evans Picture Library)

Classical and modern: Charterhouse and Westminster. Charterhouse School as it appeared in Thackeray's time, c.1840 (reproduced by permission of the BBC Hulton Picture Library) and modern languages taught by gramophone at Westminster (reproduced by permission of the Mary Evans Picture Library)

Cannon Fodder. Field Day at Eton (reproduced by permission of the BBC Hulton Picture Library)

The Field Marshal spotting military talent. Inspection of the Marlborough Cadet Force by Field Marshal Viscount Allenby (reproduced by permission of the BBC Hulton Picture Library)

'Alas, regardless of their doom, the little victims play!' Boys swimming in the Thames with Eton in the background (reproduced by courtesy of the Trustees of the Victoria and Albert Museum)

The Ring of Honour. Illustration from *Tom Brown's Schooldays* (reproduced by permission of the Mary Evans Picture Library)

Ode on a Distant Prospect
of Eton College

Ye distant spires, ye antique towers,
That crown the watry glade,
Where grateful Science still adores
Her Henry's holy shade;
And ye, that from the stately brow
Of Windsor's heights th'expanse below
Of grove, of lawn, of mead survey,
Whose turf, whose shade, whose flowers among
Wanders the hoary Thames along
His silver-winding way.

Ah happy hills, ah pleasing shade,
Ah fields belov'd in vain,
Where once my careless childhood stray'd,
A stranger yet to pain!
I feel the gales, that from ye blow,
A momentary bliss bestow,
As waving fresh their gladsome wing,
My weary soul they seem to soothe,
And redolent of joy and youth,
To breathe a second spring.

Say, father THAMES, for thou hast seen
Full many a sprightly race
Disporting on thy margent green
The paths of pleasure trace,
Who foremost now delight to cleave
With pliant arm thy glassy wave?

The captive linnet which enthrall?
What idle progeny succeed
To chase the rolling circle's speed,
Or urge the flying ball?

While some on earnest business bent
Their murm'ring labours ply
'Gainst graver hours, that bring constraint
To sweeten liberty:
Some bold adventurers disdain
The limits of their little reign,
And unknown regions dare descry:
Still as they run they look behind,
They hear a voice in every wind,
And snatch a fearful joy.

Gay hope is theirs by fancy fed,
Less pleasing when possest;
The tear forgot as soon as shed,
The sunshine of the breast:
Theirs buxom health of rosy hue,
Wild wit, invention ever-new,
And lively chear of vigour born;
The thoughtless day, the easy night,
The spirits pure, the slumbers light,
That fly th' approach of morn.

Alas, regardless of their doom,
The little victims play!
No sense have they of ills to come,
Nor care beyond to-day:
Yet see how all around 'em wait
The Ministers of human fate,
And black Misfortune's baleful train!
Ah, shew them where in ambush stand
To seize their prey the murth'rous band!
Ah, tell them, they are men!

These shall the fury Passions tear,
The vultures of the mind,
Disdainful Anger, pallid Fear,
And Shame that sculks behind;
Or pineing Love shall waste their youth,
Or Jealousy with rankling tooth,
That inly gnaws the secret heart,
And Envy wan, and faded Care,
Grim-visag'd comfortless Despair,
And Sorrow's piercing dart.

Ambition this shall tempt to rise,
Then whirl the wretch from high,
To bitter Scorn a sacrifice,
And grinning Infamy.
The stings of Falshood those shall try,
And hard Unkindness' alter'd eye,
That mocks the tear it forc'd to flow;
And keen Remorse with blood defil'd,
And moody Madness laughing wild
Amid severest woe.

Lo, in the vale of years beneath
A griesly troop are seen,
The painful family of Death,
More hideous than their Queen:
This racks the joints, this fires the veins,
That every labouring sinew strains,
Those in the deeper vitals rage:
Lo, Poverty, to fill the band,
That numbs the soul with icy hand,
And slow-consuming Age.

To each his suff'rings: all are men,
Condemn'd alike to groan,
The tender for another's pain;
Th' unfeeling for his own.
Yet ah! why should they know their fate?
Since sorrow never comes too late,

And happiness too swiftly flies.
Thought would destroy their paradise.
No more; where ignorance is bliss,
'Tis folly to be wise.

Author's Note

Everything which follows is fact. But from love of the quick and fear of the dead I have redeployed some facts and draped others in the camouflage of discretion.

S.R.

A T MY SCHOOL, Charterhouse, we never said '*Adsum*' – 'I
am here' – but '*Sum*' for short: 'I am.' Sheer idleness, I
suppose, though I myself like to think of it as being an assertion of
individual existence and personality (cf. 'I Am That I Am', or
'*Cogito ergo Sum*'). However that may be, when the roll was called
at Charterhouse in my time, we answered '*Sum*'; in the early
morning and again at the end of the day '*Sum*' rippled down the
row of faces along the panelled wall, in my House and all the other
Houses on the hill above Godalming ('Godge'). '*Sum*': 'I am.' Oh,
indeed? And who were we? If you care to follow me down the row
of faces along the panelled wall – not only at Charterhouse but in
many other schools in England where similar declarations were
made night and morning (if not of individuality, at least of
presence) – we may perhaps find out.

A T THE AGE of seven and a half, I became aware of *The Gem* and *The Magnet*. These papers came out weekly, were about forty (double-columned) pages long, and contained in every issue a story of some 20,000 words, dramatically illustrated in black and white, about the boys at two Public Schools, Saint James's (or St Jim's) in *The Gem* and Greyfriars in *The Magnet*. The stories, almost all of which about either school were written by the late Frank Richards (who lived comfortably in the South of France on the proceeds), were brisk, well constructed, exciting, totally convincing (to a seven and a half year old), and, as one was later (not much later) to learn, totally unreal.

There was, for example, the memorable story of Tom Merry in the Shell at St Jim's. Tom lent the school cad a fiver, so that the school cad (Coker) might put it on a 'dead cert' at 5 to 1 and win the £25 he needed to settle with the local money lender who was threatening him, and then restore the original fiver to Tom (no betting tax in those days). This had come from the Junior Cricket Fund, and Tom the Treasurer had consented to hand it over, not because of Coker the cad's plausible assurance that the horse (The Scarlet Marquis, if I remember) could not lose, but out of pity at Coker's lachrymose protests, that if he were reported by the money lender and then expelled the disgrace would kill his dear old parents ('Oh, Merry, I mean the world to them').

The horse loses. On the same day Fatty Wayne of the Fourth splits the best pair of Junior Batting Gloves. With happy voices the boys proclaim that Tom can go into the nearby town and buy a new pair ('in time for the match against St Bede's on Satter') with the money in the Junior Cricket Fund. Only of course, as Tom alone knows, there now is none: The Scarlet Marquis has seen to that.

[3]

To-day is Wednesday. The new gloves must be procured by Satter. Wearily Tom plods through the dreaming little town of Axbury, seeking, in vain, for a shop that sells batting gloves on credit. But what is this? It is the mid-summer fair, and bang in the middle of it a wrestling and boxing booth, the proprietor of which is offering Five Pounds to anyone who can stand up to the Brixton Bruiser for five minutes. Head high, eyes clear, lips set, Tom enters the ring.

You've guessed it. He lasts the five minutes – but not before we have had some superb narrative of the Bruiser's odious boasting before the bout begins, the backhander he tries to deliver as honest Tom goes forward to shake hands when the bell goes, his essays in murderous rabbit punches and ball bursters, his breath (even fouler than his lingo), and of the proprietor's attempt to let the fight continue after the five minutes stipulated, an attempt foiled by a pink-faced farmer with a large silver hunter. After the sporting English crowd has compelled the scented and snarling proprietor (a Wop) to hand over the prize, Tom returns in triumph with the batting gloves and makes 100 not out against St Bede's on Satter.

'Well played, young 'un,' calls Kildare, Head of the Sixth, Captain of the School, Keeper of the Stumps, Warden of the Goals (etc, etc), 'jolly well played.'

Kildare flexes his ashplant, which he carries everywhere in anticipation of *ad hoc* whackings, places it under his arm, tweaks Tom's ear, and strolls away over Junior Cricker, little knowing and never to know how near his young favourite has come to calamity.

If we forget the things that Richards has quite simply got wrong (e.g., what money lender would ever advance money to a school-boy?) and if we are prepared to ignore gross snobbery and xenophobia, we are left with an absolutely cracking yarn, immaculately paced and timed, and gorgeously, thrillingly presented.

Tom Merry was from St Jim's. It is only when we move on to Greyfriars that the highest excellence of Richard's invention is apparent: Billy Bunter, the Fat Owl of the Remove, so famous a

[4]

figure even now that he needs neither introduction nor description from me. George Orwell apostrophizes Bunter as a magnificent creation, a character on whom the sun never set, known (both to officers and men) wherever the Union Jack or the White Ensign was unfurled; Bunter, the bilker that lurks in all of us, the con-artist, the social climber, the guzzler, the sycophant, the very spirit of crapula, Bunter buffoon and butt, toady, freeloader and screaming funk. However, in the same essay in which he extols the skill and vigour that went into Bunter, Orwell blows the whistle on Frank Richards.

Richards, says Orwell, is deliberately contriving a fantasy world in order to pander to the yearning of young 'mechanicals' and shop-assistants to become part of the easy, privileged and colour-ful world in which Tom Merry is tweaked by Kildare, Bunter debagged by Harry Wharton (the clean-cut juvenile lead at Greyfriars) or roundly whipped by Quelch (the Master of the Remove). So much, says Orwell, did adolescent boys (and girls) of the lower-middle class cherish this fantasy world that many of them began to regard Tom Merry, Harry Wharton and Bunter as real people. Letters were written to them c/o The Editorial Office. One correspondent asked Kildare to write and tell him how to reach St Jim's by train and bus, and added that he would much appreciate a chat when he got there 'if this isn't too much of a cheek'. When Bob Cherry of Greyfriars was removed to the School San with mumps, books, food-parcels and even flowers were sent by his admirers. To be sure, there was a problem here, mooted by one devotee in a letter to Harry Wharton: 'Why are none of you boys ever promoted to a higher form? Why do you never get any older?' In fact a bit of promotion had been tried out by Richards: Frank Nugent of the Remove was once promoted to the Lower Fifth, but both he and his fans were so unhappy about his new status that he immediately had to revert – an interesting episode, demonstrating that although readers were almost pas-sionately anxious to regard Wharton & Co. as real people, they nevertheless resented any change or condition that might be imposed by the demands of reality. For when all was said, reality,

[5]

in the form of the inexorable necessities of a narrow and grimy world, was with them every day of their lives; they aspired to Greyfriars and St Jim's for escape, and so the more they could actually believe in these institutions, the better; but at the same time, since they all knew very well that they would never get near either, there was no need to be too literal in analysing the arrangements there.

My own fascination with these tales, though in many ways different, bore a strong resemblance to that of the apprentices and so forth whom we have just been discussing. The difference was that while they were hankering for what they would never get and were in most cases already too old to have, I was trying to anticipate a form of existence which I knew, as an upper-middle class boy of seven, was bound to come my way in six years or so. And it was a form of existence for which I longed. Most children dread the prospect of leaving home; I could hardly wait to get out. Prep. School, for which I was booked in a year or so, would be wonderful, I thought, as far as it went, but it would be altogether too small, too young and too jejune. What I wanted was a full-blooded world of flogging, feud, intrigue and fraud, of banquets at tuck shops, rebellions in the dorm, alarums, imbroglio and poisoned cups. In this I was at one with the older readers of *The Gem* and *The Magnet*, and in this lies the resemblance between their crush on Greyfriars and St Jim's and my own: but in my case, since I was actually going to go to a public school (my name was already down for Charterhouse), I was very keen to know to what extent such places really offered the thrilling *esprit* and circumstance of the Frank Richards schools, the society of Tom Merry, the *nonpareil*, of Coker the Rotter and of Billy Bunter, the all-purpose scab.

And so, while the young and deprived banausics were prepared to swallow the thing whole (while straining at the occasional gnat), my own need was to know just how accurate the picture was. Could it be true (oh, how I longed for it to be) that at Charterhouse as at St Jim's they had a carefully graded scale of penalties that ranged from fifty lines of Latin, up through a form-master's caning on the palm of the hand, a house-master's caning on the bum, a beating administered by the Headmaster himself, a Flogging (i.e. with a *birch*) by the Headmaster, a *Public* Flogging by the Headmaster, outright Expulsion, Flogging *and* Expulsion, and (oh joy, oh rapture) more and most of all, a Public Flogging followed by PUBLIC EXPULSION of the culprit? It seemed to me that the very existence of such a scale must guarantee hourly interest and daily drama ('Cherry, take a *thousand* lines' – 'Bunter, hold out your hand; wretched boy, it is encrusted with bullseyes'); and the thought of attending a Public Flogging (with or without a Public Expulsion to follow) made me quite weak with yearning.

Or again: was it the case, at Charterhouse as at St Jim's, that masters wore gowns, bands, hoods and mortar-boards every second of the day? that the Head of the School, like Kildare, had a whole XI of personal fags, at least five of which accompanied him on all his excursions in case they should be needed for sudden chores or messages? that the ghosts of starved scholars or love-lorn beaks appeared punctually every December? that as a rule the boys arranged to spend their holidays together to avoid going home to their dismal parents? that if you got a hundred runs or a hat trick you were chaired head-high round the Quad?

I could hardly wait to find out. Although I was firm in my mind that what Richards wrote was fiction and had therefore been arranged and slanted to suit his convenience and his readers' tastes, at that time I imagined (without benefit of Orwell) that most of his readers were boys of my own age, class and situation, and that therefore Richards would not dare exaggerate too grossly in matters of custom and conduct lest we should later find him out and rend him. Anyway, like all boys of that age, I was credulous, prone to believe what I was told, particularly in print; and after all, why *shouldn't* this public school world of Richards' be substantially the same as the true one? My father had confirmed that there had been whippings and mutinies, fat boys and rotters and tuck shops, lordly prefects and academically shrouded ushers, during his time at Repton; and as far as he knew, he said, the proceedings there were still pretty much the same . . . though perhaps there might have been a slight change in style. Very well, I said: could I take it that *my* school, when I got to it, would be like St Jim's or Greyfriars, though perhaps Eton jackets would be on the way out? Well, my father said: there were, there just were, certain aspects of school life that were not featured in *The Gem* and *The Magnet* . . . but about these I would find out for myself. What, I demanded, were they? I would find out in good time, my father said. Why could I not be told now? Very well, said my father, who enjoyed a sly joke: I might care to notice that no reference was ever made to how the boys at Greyfriars and St Jim's were paid for, or to the torments of the *Pater Familias* who had to squeeze out the fees, to say nothing of extras. Oh well, I said: if *that* was the only omission . . . My father muttered something about the Fruit of the Tree and then, evading, as always, the crucial issue, announced that he must be off to play squash, and repeated that sooner or later I would find out for myself.

And so, of course, I did. Meanwhile, there was I at seven and a half imagining that I would be bound, at thirteen, for a world of mortar-boards, cricket and toppers (at least on Sundays), of muffins at tea time, of splendid hierarchy and hilarious japes, a world in which every fag call heralded a theatrical flogging, a jolly outing, a sinister or thrilling adventure. A world, for all its brawling and malingering, of great innocence: there were no bullies in it, no struggle for place or power (for, despite occasional revolt, Kildare, the prefects and the beaks were fixed as firmly as Jove, and everybody knew it), no moral blackmail, false unction or social hypocrisy; and, of course, no lust: for even Coker, the Cad and the Rotter, did not masturbate in the school lavatory, nor Bunter present his ripe posterior to Smythe-Skelton, the Sybarite of the Sixth.

A YEAR LATER, when I was over eight and a half and had arrived at my Preparatory School, my views began to change, not very radically at first but enough to make for doubt. The trouble appeared to be this: although all authorities hitherto consulted (Mummy, Daddy, Nanny and Frank Richards) had broadly concurred in hailing the public school as *a good thing*, there were, it appeared, dissentient voices. Some were hostile to the public school on the ground that it was snobbish or exclusive; some damned the code and curriculum it purveyed as irrelevant and out of date; some (I remember a poisonous article in the *Daily Mirror* illustrated by a cartoon of a smirking skull with an old school tie round its neck) were clearly actuated by sheer spite.

A good example of the first class of objector was provided by one of my godfathers, a barrister called Isaak Stern, a very old friend and probably (I think now) a former lover of my mother. Isaak had been a day boy at a minor public school in the North of London, I can never remember whether it was Highgate or Mill Hill. No more could anybody else, and here was the start of all the trouble. Isaak was fiercely proud of whichever it was, wearing the old boys' tie, turning up for reunions, following the school's record for games (though he himself had scarcely put hand or foot to leather) in the sporting columns of *The Daily Telegraph*. It therefore enraged him that, whenever he answered the question 'And where did you go, Stern?', his interrogator always looked as if he were on the verge of saying '*Where?*' and only restraining himself out of kindness or good manners. This was the snobbishness which Isaak resented; *not* (as is usually the case and might well have been here) the snobbery or disdain which his own school displayed at his own expense, but that which other schools displayed at the expense of his, which he defended to the last ditch. And yet Stern (as he used to tell my mother) had had a horrible time there: squat, swarthy, quintessentially 'Jewy' (to adopt the boys' lingo) in appearance, he was nick-named 'Schmottie', persecuted by all boys from the age of twelve to twenty (in those days thick twenty-year-olds some-times lingered on at school to fail yet once more in Little-Go or Responsions), and either ignored or viciously snubbed by every

[9]

master he sat under. Nor was this a matter (*pace* his sobriquet) of anti-Semitism; there were far too many other Jews there for it to be that; it was straight snobbery caused (not least among the other Jews) by the fact that Isaak's father's occupation was collecting the cash from slot machines.

How this excellent man managed to save enough money to send Isaak to Highgate/Mill Hill is an interesting matter for conjecture but need not detain us here. Certainly, Isaak repaid his father for his sacrifice: despite the obstacles wilfully and malignantly set in his way by the entire establishment of Mill Hill/Highgate, he achieved an Exhibition to Trinity Hall in Cambridge . . . whither he went and where he first met my mother, who grew up there, early in the twenties. One evening, when my mother remarked that the new husband of her best friend had been at the same school as Isaak and then named whichever of the two it was that Isaak hadn't been to, she received a long scolding for her error, and was told that such confusion was typical of the snobbishness of the English middle and public school classes, who disdained a school attended in part by day boys. There followed an exegesis on the shameful attitudes exhibited, at Trinity Hall, by Etonians, Rugbeians, Sherbornians, Tonbridgeans and even Brightonians towards Mill Hill/Highgate, which was as good a school, when it came to fundamentals, as any of them. That it should be patronised, looked down upon, despised and even hated by supposedly grander schools not only indicated the hideous defects of the system but both heralded and explained its imminent decay or abolition.

'Who's going to abolish it?' my mother said (or so she told me many years later).

'People like me, who have been humiliated by it.'

'I see. Because you were bullied at a wretched little school like ——,' said my mother, naming the wrong one, 'you would like to destroy all public schools whatever, including the very best of them.'

'*Especially* what you call the very best of them. It is those that have crucified ****,' said Isaak, naming the right one, 'and boys from those that have mocked and insulted me for having gone there. Please let us get this straight: I am *not* complaining about my treatment at ****, only about the treatment that has been meted out to me by Harrovians and the rest because I *went* to ****.'

'But why *aren't* you complaining about your treatment at ****?' my mother said. 'Since I have known you you have done nothing but tell me skin-flaying stories of what happened to you there. There was the time when someone put boracic acid in the pot of stuff you carried about for your spots, and the time when your ink-well during an exam was filled with invisible ink, and the time when your mother and father came to the School Concert and there was a whole four-minute sketch about a man who collected the money from slot machines, oh and far worse, the time when they got you at bayonet point on Field Day and made you drink a bottle of Californian Syrup of Figs straight down, and the time when you went to change to go home and found that someone had done number two in your out-door shoes . . .'

'. . . Only been sick. Don't exaggerate. The malice was improvised and not pre-planned, and was therefore venial . . .'

'. . . And the time they put a Roman Candle up your bum and then lit it and waited for it to explode.'

'It was the kind that didn't explode.'

'*They* didn't know that. How *can* you say,' said my mother, 'that you resent being despised as an ——ian . . .'

'. . . As an ****ian . . .'

'. . . But don't resent the foul things they did to you at ——.'

'****. My dear . . . one cannot repudiate an establishment which one has represented, on several occasions, both in honourable defeat and memorable victory, on the field of play.'

'*Field of play?* You couldn't lift a football off the ground without falling flat on your face.'

'No. But I am a passable performer at Chess.'

And out it came. Uncle Isaak (as my brother and I used to call him) had played Chess for ****. He had even been, on one occasion, acting Vice Captain. No amount of snobbishness,

malice or intrigue could prevent his being included in the side –
nor indeed did anyone wish to prevent it, as Chess was held in such
general contempt at **** that Isaak's membership of the team was
simply one more nail with which to crucify him. But to Isaak it was
a proud thing to be selected to represent one's school at the most
ancient game of them all; and having not only played Chess for
**** but having in due course been awarded his Chess Colours, he
could never, being the man he was, breathe a word in denigration
of the academy by which he had been thus honoured.

Yet he remained a trenchant critic of the public school system as
a whole. As I have indicated above, I first began to realise that not
everyone thought the public schools an unmixed blessing when I
was about eight and a half and had just begun to attend a
preparatory school; and indeed it was Uncle Isaak, a genial and
generous godfather (though an unofficial one, I suppose, since he
was a Jew) and a very amusing companion who was the first (in my
experience) to sound a note of dissent. His charge, as we have
heard, was that the older and more famous public schools looked
down on the others. Now, the fairly lengthy and elaborate account
of his attitude which I have given above is based on conversations
(between him and my mother, between my mother and me, and
between Isaak and me) held over many years; but when I first
heard him speak on the topic, newly home from my first summer
term at my prep. school, his complaint was absolutely clear and
direct, with no personal reference.

'The thing is,' he said, 'that these places were mostly founded to
educate poor local boys who had shown ability. Then the rich got
into the act. Here, they realised, was a good thing going cheap –
nothing a rich man likes better than bargain prices. What was
more, it got your trouble-making children out of the way for most
of the year . . . very handy this, as the old way of doing it – sending
'em as pages to another rich man's castle – was just going out of
fashion. So they used their influence to hog the vacancies or make
extra ones at all the most conveniently situated foundations; and
from then on, where you should have had poor humble boys who
were grinding away at their Latin Grammar (on which they

depended for their livelihood), you now had the idle and flashy sons of great merchants and noblemen, who knew that they were being *dumped* and resented it. So what did they do? They took it out on such of the poor scholars who were still around the place, and then, when they had more or less dispossessed them altogether, took it out on the grammar schools (i.e. those schools which for one reason or another had never appealed to rich parents and therefore hadn't grown smart like Eton or Winchester) in which the poor scholars took refuge. Then, in the nineteenth century, a whole lot of new public schools were set up to supply empire-builders, and of course these were despised by the old lot almost more than the grammar schools were . . . because, whereas the grammar schools were absolutely genuine in their own kind, the new public schools were just shoddy imitations of the grand ones. 'But you are not to think,' Isaak used to say as we pottered about the summer landskip, 'that this last fact *excuses* the famous schools for taking such attitudes toward the weaker ones. The assumption of superiority is the most offensive thing in the sight of God.'

How closely I followed Uncle Isaak, I no longer remember; but I certainly got his drift, and most profoundly disagreed with it. If you knew you were better than something or somebody else, why should you not recognise the fact? A little modesty might of course be seemly, and exhibitions of disdain were certainly uncalled for, but what Uncle Isaak seemed to be questioning, in the end, was the right of the great schools even to consider themselves superior to, e.g., ****.

Nearly fifty years later, with the benefit of hindsight, I think I understand what caused Uncle Isaak's almost obscene resentment: the fusion of the two strongest elements in his nature.

For the first great point about Uncle Isaak was his loyalty. Loyalty, as we have seen, to ****; and loyalty to England. A few years later, when the 1939 war began, Uncle Isaak instantly volunteered. He need not have done: he was by then drawing near to middle age and he was, as he always had been, physically inept. He was doing a useful job where he was, and so they told him;

what was more, they said, there was no job in khaki for him. But there was a job, it seemed, in Air Force Blue: more clerks were needed in the legal department of the RAF: squat Uncle Isaak could certainly fill that bill.

'Aircraftsman Stern,' mused my mother when he told her the news.

Well – er – not quite. There had been a little change: Aircraftsman Strang, Aircraftsman Iain Strang. Isaak and Stern were well-known Jewish names, and if the Gestapo should ever arrive in force in this country their unhappy owner might be speedily suppressed.

'But Isaak, dear,' my mother said: 'don't you think that even as Iain Strang you might be . . . well . . . spotted?'

'What do you mean?' he said.

'Well . . . your appearance is, to say the least of it, a little Levantine.'

'That I am short, fat and dark need not necessarily mean that I am a Jew.'

And here of course was the second strong element in Uncle Isaak's – I mean Uncle Iain's – character: a streak of almost hysterical velleity. Once play Chess for your school, however appalling that school may be, and everything becomes all right, the school a noble pile and you its shining knight. Change your name from Isaak Stern to Iain Strang, and no one will ever know you are Jewish. (The fallacy is comparable to that of the Hellenophile Jews in the 2nd Century BC, who, before going down to exercise naked in the gymnasium, clipped on false foreskins to make themselves Greek.)

So: loyalty on the one hand, velleity on the other. If you wish to be loyal to the school that has spurned and abused you, you find excuse for it, you somehow fudge the issue, by claiming that the school itself is really the wronged party because *it* has been spurned and abused by other schools that arrogate superior status. You re-distribute the burden of blame, so to speak, you absolve your school of its guilt by spreading the load on other schools, by indicting the entire system.

[14]

This may (or may not) have been the clue to Uncle Isaak's curious inconsistency. It is always possible, of course, that I am making it all too complicated – that in simple truth Uncle Isaak just enjoyed being perverse. For a perverse man he certainly was: having insured his life in case of German invasion by becoming (as he thought) a gentile, he then gravely imperilled it again, six months later, by marrying a Rabbi's daughter. I suppose loyalty got the better of him here: after all, his denial of kith with Jewry smacked most grievously of treachery and anti-Semitism; perhaps he might be forgiven (velleity) if he took to his bosom the spectacularly vain and repugnant daughter (so my mother reported) of one of Jewry's priests. Whether this calculation would have been that of Uncle Isaak or Uncle Iain is not quite clear to me, but in either event it turned out to have been correct; for as Iain Strang, the Rabbi's son-in-law, he now prospered, being not so long afterwards gazetted as a Squadron Leader in the Legal Department of the RAF and being, at the end of the war, triumphantly elected as the President of the Finchley Chess Club.

I T SEEMS TO ME, at this stage, that some comment is called for on the prevalence of anti-Semitism in British Public Schools. The subject is vast, volatile and rebarbative: for myself, lacking detailed knowledge, I can only render the impression which I have received from wide if desultory reading, from the oral reports of the few friends or contemporaries whom I know to be tolerably exact in other matters and may therefore assume to be so in this, and from my own experience as a public schoolboy in the nineteen-forties.

Debate and discussion, in this area, are unfortunately dominated by two extreme parties: by the party that sees anti-Semitism writhing and coiling like a cancer through the entire public school system; and the party that blandly maintains it is so little known as to be negligible. My own memory, supplemented by the sources mentioned above, tells me that anti-Semitism was an established fact in public schools before, during and after my own day, but that it was governed (if not discouraged) by certain limiting and salutary conventions.

The first of these conventions, the official reason (as it were) for hating the Jews, lingered long but has been so heavily discredited any time since (say) 1920 that it can hardly be said to have operated after that date *except* in odd and isolated alcoves. This is the convention that the Jews were responsible for the Crucifixion. A Jewish friend of mine, innocently enquiring of his Tutor at Eton in 1942 why the Jews were so widely hated, was roundly told, 'Because, boy, the Jews butchered Jesus Christ'; but this dominie was wretchedly out of date in his assumptions (a) that the Jews (rather than the Romans) were indeed the assassins, (b) that anyone still cared whether they were or not, and (c) that people could not distinguish between the few Jewish contemporaries of Christ who might *perhaps* have murdered him and those living nearly 2,000 years later, who had plainly had no hand in the thing. In short, then, except in highly peculiar quarters, that cock don't fight any longer, and hasn't for at least fifty years.

The second conventional excuse for despising the Jews, and for sometimes actually maltreating them, was that some of them looked so awful, particularly when adolescent. 'Why must you look so *Jewy*?' some of us would say to a shambling, dirty, scrofulous Jewish clown, who had a way of wolfing all the (rationed) potatoes at lunch when no one else was looking. The short answer was, of course, that the poor fellow, as kindly, generous and intelligent a boy as you'd meet in a week's march, simply could not help it and should in all decency have been at once forgiven on that ground alone. But the trouble was that a combination of the most distressing features of underfed and overgrown pubescence with such Levantine characteristics as blubber lips, bulbous nostrils and greasy black hair was so appalling that all instincts of decency in the beholder were from time to time wiped out. A protest was due, one felt, if only on aesthetic grounds. And so in the mass we occasionally – I repeat, occasionally – went in for Jew-baiting. Later on, one by one, we would creep up to the trembling, battered creature and make our separate apologies: 'I'm sorry, Priseman,' I for my part would say, 'but I couldn't go against all the rest of them, could I?' May God forgive me.

Another convention in all this was that Jews were always 'Jewing' one. They had a way of getting better or best, of over-reaching, and they must (one felt) be cut back. In practice, this feeling took the form of spiteful resentment of any Jew who achieved academic or athletic success along with denigration of his achievement. I remember two very skilful Jewish slow bowlers, who were constantly accused of 'Jewing people out with your Jewy leg breaks'. And then there was the interesting and scandalous instance of a Head of the School who tried to persuade the Captain of Cricket to omit a particularly 'Jewy'-looking Jew from the 1st XI for the match against Eton. ('It don't look good playing that sort of cove against Eton.') Whether or not the Captain of Cricket would have yielded in this affair we never found out, because the Jewish boy in question had to go away to take some exam and so was not available for the match.

Oddly enough, *money* played no part here. It was generally realised that many Jewish boys were the sons of rich men, who, we might have assumed, had got their loot through 'Jewing'. But for some reason we never thought in these terms: I suppose that the sort of world, in which that sort of money was made, was too far removed from our experience or comprehension to concern us. Such anti-Semitic grudges as we had were strictly practical and immediate. They were not, as I have said, based on religious grounds or on indignation about the Crucifixion, or even on a distaste for a particular race (though sometimes our way of expressing ourselves suggested such a distaste): they were an immediate reaction to extreme ugliness of a kind unfamiliar to Anglo-Saxons (normal or 'English' ugliness was tolerated and sometimes prized), or the nasty but not very harmful results of

[17]

envy of superior ability – an envy which we allowed ourselves to indulge openly if its object were Jewish but must at all cost suppress if he were not.

Whether there are any general conclusions to be drawn from these remarks, I am uncertain. If there are, they might take the following form:

(a) Most human beings, since they are of very poor quality, long to find someone of even poorer quality than themselves to abuse and stamp on. The Jews, being people of doubtful origin, alien custom and often distasteful appearance (at least to an Anglo-Saxon eye), being also of diffident and gentle manners, seem ideal for this purpose.

(b) When, therefore, the Jews persistently demonstrate, by their moral steadfastness and versatile performance, that they are undisputably superior (in many respects at least) to their mean-spirited detractors, they are envied with the most virulent envy of all, the consequences of which have been lethal in many circumstances, but in a civilised and well-supervised establishment (e.g. a school) generally go little further than spiteful belittlement of the worth or truth of their endeavours.

S LIGHTLY LATER than I learned from Uncle Isaak that it was, after all, possible to disapprove of the public schools and what was one (his) of the possible grounds, I also became aware of another line of inimical approach. The public schools, according to this second indictment, were teaching the wrong subjects, the wrong values, and the wrong way to behave.

The subject is vast and labyrinthine. Luckily I can compress a useful study of it into the story of just one man: Mr George Nicholas Opington, who taught French and mathematics on a very junior level at my preparatory school, but reserved his real enthusiasm for carpentry, natural history, practical forestry and path-making – 'pioneering', as he used to sum the whole package.

Mr Opington had not got a degree. He had run away from Haileybury at the age of sixteen and a half, 'listed as a boy soldier, sickened of it, and bought himself out with the proceeds of a small legacy . . . with the remainder of which he then purchased a passage to New Zealand, where he walked the three islands from end to end, occasionally working as a casual labourer or doing rather formidable odd jobs (such as re-roofing a shed or making a farm-hands' refectory table) at which he became more and more proficient.

At length he chanced to be harboured for a couple of nights in a forester's lodge, found himself fascinated by the forester's current investigation into sources of sylvan disease, and somehow contrived to be appointed as the man's companion and deputy at a nominal salary. Now followed seven or eight years of incessant travel through the forests of New Zealand, until one day he returned to base from a lengthy expedition to be told that his father had died suddenly, apparently leaving his mother homeless. When he had last heard from them six months before, his father had been a prosperous underwriter and the couple had been living in the Sunningdale house which the family had occupied ever since he could remember. Plainly something had gone very wrong indeed and home he went to find out what.

The story was commonplace. His father had been speculating heavily on the Stock Exchange and had been close to total failure when he died of a heart attack. Everything there was, including the house, had had to go to settle his commitments, and his wife, Mr Opington's mother, was now living with her elder sister, a graceless and self-righteously solvent old maid. Mr Opington now did the correct thing. Although he had scarcely seen his mother in fifteen years (ever since he ran off from Haileybury followed by family execration) he had preserved for her an at least theoretical affection and he now decided that he owed it to her (if only just) to save her from her atrocious sister. Although his salary in New Zealand had been tiny, his expenditure had been almost nil and his savings would run to a small cottage somewhere. As for work, he applied for advice to the Headmaster of his old preparatory school, always an ally even after he bolted from Haileybury, and was recommended by him to another Headmaster, who had a vacancy and knew a good thing when he saw it. So Mr Opington, appointed to teach French, mathematics, carpentry, etc, at Cordwalles School near Camberley in the County of Surrey, moved his old mother into a bungalow among the pines on the edge of the school grounds and settled to his new career.

And hated it. The Surrey pines were no substitute for the wilds of New Zealand. He did not very much like boys. He was bored by his mother. He was appalled by the curriculum and disciplinary system of Cordwalles, which reproduced on a prep. school level everything that he had most resented about Haileybury. Nothing in English private education seemed to have changed in the very slightest, he found, during the sixteen odd years since he had last suffered under it. How gladly he would have departed; but he was trapped – trapped by his mother, by lack of money, by lack of official qualification (despite his experience in New Zealand, the British Forestry Commission wouldn't look at him), by lack of social connections, by a sense of obligation to the man who had given him his job, by the need or at least the preference (old-fashioned even then) to lie low until the scandal of his father's failure had died away.

And this was his situation (so he told me many years later) in May of 1936, when he had been at Cordwalles for three years and I had just arrived to begin my first term. He was still only just over thirty-five, eager to be gone, compelled to stay, beginning to rot, consoled only by the occasional opportunity to tend the trees on the school estate . . . and, as we shall see, by his 'cello. All I knew of him then was the same as everyone else knew of him, that he taught 'Frog', maths and 'carpy', also 'birds and bugs' and forestry (though very little space was found for either on the timetable of Cordwalles), that he played and taught no game, that his manner, while never discourteous, tended to the morose, that he had an old 'mater' in a 'prole-hutch' in the woods – and that he had recently taken up the violoncello. It must have been during the Easter hols, said an older boy; there had been no 'cello last term. There was now, and of it we had vivid experience. For the mater, it seemed, refused to let him practise the instrument in the prole-hutch, so he used to play it, instead, in the empty gymnasium. Every evening from eight till nine or later an appalling permutation of mee-aws and grunts would drift up to the roof of the gym, out of the ventilators, across the front lawn, and into the open windows of the boys' dormitories.

'Opie's farting,' we all said. 'Opie is a fat pig.'

Which was unkind but not altogether unfair. Deprived of his treks through the forest, Mr Opington was running, very fast, to fat. And indeed it was this misfortune which led, if only indirectly, to the first exposition – the first of many – which I heard from him on the grievous academic and ethical faults of the public school system.

It happened during 'carpy'. I was no good at this; I had no eye for grain or line, no hand for plane or chisel; I was just thoroughly clumsy. Bored with my task, humiliated by the hideous mess I had just made of a hole intended to receive a joint – it was meant to be square and had come out heptagonal – I seized the deformed leg of the stool which I was supposed to be constructing and wrote on it, in sheer disgust and desperation,

CARPY IS SILLY MUCK AND FAT OPIE AND HIS FARTING
CELLO OUGHT TO BE IN A FREAK SHOW

Yes; I was a nasty and inventive little boy.

This was clearly what Mr Opington thought when he came round to me ten minutes later. But being the man he was he was more interested in my powers of invention than hurt or shocked by my nastiness. As he approached I became more and more appalled by what I had written (in red and green, with my four-colour propelling pencil). I tried to hide the offending limb; but three legs were not enough to pass Opie's inspection. The fourth was required of me and carefully examined. There was a long thoughtful silence – but no blow, no chit to the Headmaster. Opie slowly

[21]

got himself into gear, then proceeded to get his own back on me by taking me on in my own terms – those of personal insult.

'Fat, am I?' he rumbled. 'Yes, I suppose I am. And you, Raven, have filthy finger-nails, smelly feet and a scab under your nose. I should not have mentioned these unappetising features to you had you not thrust my obesity at me. We do not, as gentlemen, go in for personal remarks. That is one of the polite understandings in which you are being educated, and a very good one too.'

He paused.

'Do you understand what I am saying?' he said.

'Yes, sir. We must make ourselves decent to each other and not talk about things which will upset other people.'

'Ah,' he said, and sat down heavily on a bench. 'But you are taking it too far. That is the whole trouble with the education you are beginning: it starts with an excellent precept – like "Don't make personal remarks" for one – and then ends by such injection of hypocrisy and prudishness that people finish up unable to make any remarks at all. The public school system, boy, will destroy your powers of judgment and your will to speak as you find.'

There was much embarrassed fidgeting in the carpentry room. We were here – most of us – to learn 'carpy', which was 'what our parents are paying for', as we might odiously have said – not to listen to Opie's dimly comprehended attack on the type of school to which we all aspired after this one. For myself, however, I was far more interested in the line of thought, though still obscure to me, that Opie was opening up than in my beastly crooked stool.

'But sir . . .' I began.

'Not now, boy,' said Opie, looking round the resentful faces; 'later if you like.'

I did like. I walked by Opie and spoke with him on the next Sunday afternoon walk which he supervised. We became friends. And this is what he told me, first in simple form during the years at Cordwalles, and then in more mature fashion later on, when I was much older and still occasionally returned to his bungalow to listen, or had letters from him wherever I might be:

'It is all a matter' (Opie said) 'of speaking the truth. The other

[22]

day in carpentry we spoke the truth of each other about small matters in an offensive way. Pointless and rude. But other things – bigger things – *must* be spoken of openly, otherwise we shall never come at any important truth.

'Now see here, boy. I have noticed from your French lessons that you are good at memorising French Grammar and constructing French sentences. This school and your next school will approve of this. They will be glad that you understand the Grammar and the Syntax. They will tolerate, perhaps even encourage, your going to France to practise them and to acquire a correct French accent. Their tolerance will cease abruptly when you read certain French books and start asking awkward questions. At this stage, just as you are approaching the truth or some part of it, they will start heading you off. That is what happened to me at Haileybury.

'As you may or may not know, Haileybury is a school originally founded by the East India Company to educate those who are to defend and administer our Empire. In order to be qualified to do this, one has to pass exams: exams into Sandhurst for soldiers; exams into universities for those seeking entry into other Services, the more important of them at any rate; exams for degrees; exams for actual acceptance by the Service in question and usually exams for promotion to higher rank within it.

'Haileybury exists in order to prepare a man for the more elementary of such exams, to be taken when one is about seventeen or eighteen.

'The subjects are various and are of very wide interest, because we in England believe, quite rightly, that a man who has received a civilised general education is better qualified to govern a province or control a police force than a man who has been narrowly reared on purely necessary and practical information. The trouble is, that one is being taught these potentially fascinating subjects – literature, history, mathematics – with a view to passing an examination in them rather than to finding out the truth behind them. Now, if a chap can pass an exam it tells you a lot about him – that he can make himself understood in decent English (French, Urdu or

[23]

whatever), in legible handwriting, despite disagreeable circumstances, shortage of time, and lack of reference books. So exams affirm the presence or the absence of many important and useful qualities, from the point of view of the Services concerned, in those that pass or fail them; but in being trained to pass an exam in a certain subject you will not be encouraged to linger on the important truths which lie behind it – indeed you will be discouraged, thwarted, diverted, warned off and finally forbidden.

'I read the Classics. I was not going into the Army or any of the Foreign or Colonial Services, I didn't indeed know what I should do. My father was rich and the world seemed open; so I read the Classics with a view to passing into Cambridge and seeing what turned up then. Meanwhile the syllabus – it was decided at an early stage that I should try for a scholarship – was demanding and altogether excellent. The trouble was the spirit in which it was taught.

'The whole of Graeco-Roman civilisation was made to appear as if it had never really existed at all, as if the entire thing had been got up in the abstract by a committee of schoolmasters, as if the languages had been invented and the history devised solely in order to provide a framework against which pupils might be mentally trained, disciplined and examined. The two languages were used to provide exercise in grammar and syntax and occasionally to give the substance for a prim essay which would rehearse the merits, as conventionally conceived, of such-and-such a poem or passage of prose and win an "alpha", from an examiner conditioned to recognise and reward such routine good form, in exchange for its social and moral propriety. The history was cast as a series of improving lessons in the demands of duty and the perils of "slackness", of misapplied "cleverness", or of any tendency to make jokes about "Serious Matters". Greek and Roman religions were, quite correctly, written off as superstitions, as superfluities or lapses of taste on the part of the originating committee: so far, so good, had it not been for the nagging insistence that Christianity, by contrast, was *not* a superstition because it had been "revealed" by "Our Lord". (And woe betide

[24]

anybody who dared to dispute the distinction.) As for ancient art, it had somehow got in on the act by mistake; the committee of schoolmasters (one might have supposed) had made a real blunder here . . . a blunder that was disguised or excused by the doctrine that Greek Statuary (when properly fig-leaved) gave us a praise-worthy example of physical fitness, showing chaps what could be made of their bodies if they used them to play healthy games and did not pamper or – er – abuse them. The study of Archaeology was also a potential embarrassment, as it encouraged the notion that the ancient world had not only existed but positively flourished in its own right; but in this case as in that of the artefacts it was somehow inculcated that whatever was dug up was in the nature of educational equipment, previously put there for the purpose of being excavated, and had nothing to do with the real if long-vanished habitation and culture of a real people.

'It was, of course, quite possible to enjoy all this if one was capable of the same kind of mental ambivalence as (e.g.) the father of Edmund Gosse, who, Gosse tells us in *Father and Son*, absolutely *knew*, as a fundamentalist, that the world had been created lock and stock in six days flat in 4004 BC, yet at the same time happily assigned his fossils or geological specimens to periods thousands and millions of years earlier. But such enjoyment I myself should have found uneasy; and to make matters worse a huge amount of material that was considered unsuitable or unassi-milable was either omitted altogether or, if that was not possible for whatever reason, most shabbily falsified.

'In short, we were being flannelled, we were being bamboozled, we were being sold.' And so I left. Just went. Silly, really. Dishonest as the teaching was, it was effective in its way and once I had made and firmly framed my own reservations I could have benefited a great deal from it. And then I should no doubt have enjoyed Cambridge. But I was young and priggish and abjured the lie at the bottom of it all. Travel was the thing, I thought: roam the world and see for yourself: find the truth that way. But since I was already disowned, my travels must be subsidised – so what about the Army? Unfortunately the Army too liked to prescribe the

[25]

answers – if not about the interpretation of Horace then about rules of acceptable conduct. So I went where nobody could prescribe any rules except myself – into the forest. Trees don't dictate and don't lie.

'But then I had to leave my trees to come back to England and look after my mother . . . which meant teaching at Cordwalles (where I first met you), which in turn meant accepting or at least tolerating the old lies again and helping to propagate them. Teaching you French and knowing that you would be turned into a proficient examinee and lied to about anything "unsound" which you might chance to read in the language – if, that is, they weren't sharp enough to prevent you reading it at all.

'Consolation I had to have; and a scattering of Surrey pines did not provide it. So in a small way I took up music. A note in music can be false if wrongly played, but it is not a lie. It declares itself as what it is for all to hear. Why the 'cello, you ask? No particular reason, except vague preference on grounds totally irrelevant to music itself. The 'cello is a companionable instrument, nice and large, with a man to man appeal; it sits comfortably between the thighs; there is nothing finicking about it; it may groan or belch or howl, but at least it doesn't squeak. Oh yes; I contrived to be quite happy by myself during those evenings in the gym; it was like some of the evenings in New Zealand, when I was bivouacking under the trees with my horse, an agreeable companion like my 'cello later on, occasionally stubborn but not given to self-righteousness or lies.'

Opie's mother died during the war and Opie some ten years after her. Though set free by his mother's death, he had been declared physically unfit to return to his old employment in New Zealand, so he had gone on living in the bungalow even after Cordwalles closed. For a time, he wrote and told me, the caretaker was quite happy to let him come and play his 'cello in the gymnasium in the evenings; but then, without any explanation other than 'Governors' orders', the place was abruptly and permanently locked up. And so, having now no mother to object, Opie played his 'cello in the bungalow, until one day one of the strings went. This had often happened before, but this time he no longer had the heart to replace it.

I FEEL that the above episode requires a brief gloss.
My friend Opington complained at some length, it may have been noted, that he was not taught the Latin and Greek Classics in an honest fashion. Now Cyril Connolly, in his brilliant preface to his dismal novel, *The Rock Pool*, writes of his own classical education (at Eton) with exactly the opposite import, explicitly stating that for his part he was so candidly instructed in his Latin and Greek texts (with particular reference here to the poets) that he absorbed the message almost at once – and subsequently underwent, from the conventional point of view, a severe decline in his moral character.

To a percipient boy as well taught as he was, Connolly maintains, the meaning of these texts was plain beyond any possibility of misunderstanding. They were urging (among other things) that all varieties of sensuous, sensual and sexual pleasure are not only delectable in themselves but also gain a poetic, an elegiac flavour from being so brief and fading so fast; that 'present joy' is 'present laughter'; that old age, which denies pleasure and insists on pain, is a sad, cruel, humiliating business, not to be much alleviated by moral dignity or religious faith; that death is the merciful end of all, and is followed neither by bliss nor torment, only by oblivion; that all moral judgments are dispensable (though in gentlemen at least we should look for public generosity, personal modesty, and, in matters of pleasure and entertainment, an elegant sense of style); that all amusements, mental or physical, are potentially good in so far as they are potentially agreeable; and that, inasmuch as the word 'virtue' has any meaning, it implies worldly wisdom and tolerance.

'He who runs may read.' Connolly, he tells us, read the message
on the run and then ran straight on into moral obloquy. His
manner, tone and assumptions, he assures us, became so distasteful to a world which, if not particularly moral, at least takes the
trouble to be hypocritical, that his work, for a time, was almost
unpublishable and definitely unassimilable by the society for
which it was intended. (What work? one asks oneself with hindsight. When did the wretch ever do any?) He was accused (and
himself joins in the accusation) of being coarse, cynical, mater-
ialistic, gluttonous, bibulous and (whenever possible – he was not
a pretty man) priapic. True, some of his sentiments, like those of
the classical authors who had made him what he was, 'were not
without elevation and melancholy', but the main insistence was on
carnal pleasure and function, on bodily flowering and decay. As
the poet Horace has it (in Louis MacNeice's translation),

> Equally heavy is the heel of white-faced death
> > on the pauper's
> Shack and the towers of Kings, and O my dear
> The little sum of life forbids the ravelling of lengthy
> Hopes. Night and the fabled dead are near
>
> And the narrow house of nothing, past whose lintel
> > You will meet no wine like this, no boy to admire
> Like Lycidas, who to-day makes young men a
> furnace
> And whom to-morrow the girls will find a fire.

Precisely. Easy come, easy go, here today and gone tomorrow,
and to hell with all your bread and water moralisers, who, for all
their cant and abstinence, are just as dead after seventy years or so
as the rest of us and then, being dead, know nothing more for good
or ill than we do.

It was this kind of thing, Connolly says, inculcated by the
reading of the classics at Eton, that made him a sort of legend of
bad taste and lack of tact ('insensitivity') with editors and the

reading public. But although he may have got no good of the message, from the public or official point of view, he had certainly *got* it, for weal or woe he had certainly got it, and got it easily too, and relished it, and very grateful he was of it, despite the prim airs and the namby-pamby complaints of the Pooters all about him.

Now, if we compare Connolly's case with Opie's, it appears that in Opie's a deliberate effort was made to keep the message (of joyous pagan immorality and intransigence) away from Opie. That this effort was not altogether successful is quite clear, if only because Opie realised that they were trying to 'bamboozle' him and rapidly departed in consequence, detesting the falseness of it all; but Opie's point, that there *was* an effort made at Haileybury to pull the wool over the eyes of himself and others, is beyond any dispute. Connolly, on the other hand, makes no complaint of this nature: at Eton, it would seem, the pagan poets, with their recommendation of transient carnal pleasures before absolute and unpunishable death, were all out in the open unopposed for six days a week, only Sunday being reserved for Christ and Jehovah, whom no one much cared for (both being Jews) in any case. The only conclusion one can come to, on the available evidence, is that Haileybury, being a 'Service' school, had at least residual Puritan tendencies and so did try to obfuscate the subversive message of (e.g.) Horace, whereas Eton and the aristocracy found Horace totally congenial and needed no damned nonsense about God . . . Who was in any event only there to put the wind up the working classes.

I HAVE SAID that when I went to Cordwalles at the age of eight and a half I was conscious, or becoming conscious, of three strains of complaint about the public schools: objection to their snobbery and exclusiveness; adverse criticism of the curriculum taught and the conduct encouraged; and pure, blind hate. Of the first two strains I have just treated: now for hate.

The odd thing is that the most ferocious hatred of the public schools is often conceived by otherwise mild and rational people. There was at Cordwalles when I first went there a jolly boy called Brian who cleaned the shoes and did odd jobs. He was sixteen years old, pleasant looking despite the half jar of Brylcreem he used daily, and agreeable to talk to, having an accent which owed more to Somerset, where he had been brought up till the age of fourteen, than to Surrey. He was given to passing his sweets out among the boys (and thus risking his job) and to enquiring in a loyal way how such and such an XI had 'ended up' on Saturday – when he occasionally spent some of his afternoon off watching part of the match.

When war was declared in 1939, he volunteered, being now well over nineteen, for the Somerset Light Infantry, and was at length notified that he must report to the Regimental Depot in Taunton on a date near the middle of the following February. This we learned when we came back for the Easter Term in the middle of January, and much was made of Brian, during the few weeks that remained to him.

Now, the Headmaster's wife, a fanatical follower of dietetic fads, had already seized on the war as an excuse for substituting watercress for butter and jam at tea ('more healthy, and it helps the war effort') even before rationing was imposed. By way of further economy, she now announced that after Brian 'had gone away to do his bit' he would not be replaced, but that the older boys would then begin 'to do *their* bit' by cleaning all the shoes seven days a week. We would now, she told us, be instructed in the art by Brian. From February 1 till February 14, the day before Brian would leave to join the Colours, we would go to him in shifts of three and learn how three boys could clean ninety pairs of shoes between six and eight-thirty p.m. When someone enquired how we were to do our prep on our shoe-cleaning evenings, he was told that we would be excused. When he pointed out that his parents were paying for him to learn the normal school subjects and not the tasks of servants, he was called a nasty and unpatriotic little boy who wouldn't even clean his own shoes to help the war effort. When he said that he was perfectly prepared to clean his own shoes but didn't see why he should clean anybody else's, he had his ears boxed. That was the way of it in those days, and it has to be said that it turned out a better sort of boy than those that are nowadays stifled by 'pastoral care' and gorged to the point of crapula by almost hourly treats.

But I digress. Brian was to teach us to clean the school's shoes, and Brian, being a conscientious young man, was determined to leave behind him a legacy of well-trained little boot blacks. While not a martinet, he was an exacting master, sparing of praise, just with blame, suffering no laxity; but he believed very firmly that there should be a five-minute break in every hour, during which he passed his sweets round and shoe cleaning was forgotten – till it must start again.

It was during one such break, on the last session of this kind that I should be attending, two days before Brian was to leave, that an inspiration to speak sooth suddenly descended on him.

'I did think,' he was saying, 'that *she* [the Headmaster's wife] might have given me a couple of days off before I went. Days off with pay, I mean. Not her.'

'How mean,' we said.

'I couldn't afford the days off without the money, and so I told *him* [the Headmaster]. *He* said he'd arrange it all, in that lah-di-dah - don't - bother - to - call - me - Jesus - Christ - even - though - you-know-I-am way of his, but nothing happened. Too scared of *her*, I wouldn't wonder.'

'Everyone's scared of *her*,' we said.

'Eunuch,' Brian said: 'no balls. Them public schools is what does it. What's that dainty tie he wears with stripes?'

'The Old Marlburian,' we said.

'Old arse-lickers, the fucking creep. Christ, how I hate those bloody places.'

'Why, Brian?' we said.

[31]

'Because they're all haw-haw voices and "After you, Cecil" and "Play the game, Claude" and "I say, spiffing shot, old bean" and "King and Country, do or die" – and then, when a chap like me's going away to perhaps do both, they won't give him a couple of days off. Or not with his money.'

'That was *her*,' we said.

'But *he* promised to speak to *her*, and he didn't.'

'He was scared, as we all said. Or perhaps *he* did speak to *her*, and *she* said "no".'

'Then he's a bigger fucking creep than ever. No proper man takes "no" from a bloody woman. If he does, he's a woman himself. That's what *those places* do to people – turn 'em into fucking pansy boys, bleeding women. That's what they'll do to you when you get there. Turn you into a lot of fucking women and ever so frightfullah lah-di-dah voices as if you was Jesus Christ forgiving everyone from off his fucking Cross.'

Pure hate. We had three minutes of it. Everything he had already said, repeated and crudely elaborated. He didn't hate us because we were going to public schools, nor did he really hate the Headmaster because he'd been to one, he just hated the schools themselves (here was no lover of *The Gem* or *The Magnet*) and what he conceived they did to their pupils, which was, in his eyes, to teach them to cheat and at the same time to condescend to people like himself, the whole operation being conducted in an 'ectuallah-ectuallah' voice with the vapours of a spineless woman.

Punctually at the end of the five-minute break he distributed a last round of sweets and set us to work again.

'No skimping,' he said: 'don't forget the crevice between the sole and the upper. I want the Headmaster and his wife to know I've done a proper job to the last.'

Later on, when we dismissed, I said to Brian,

'Where did you get those ideas about the public schools? They're not quite like that, you know.'

'Ever been to one, Raven?'

Brian called us all by our surnames.

'No, but . . .'

[32]

'. . . I have. My mother and father were servants in one of the houses on the boys' side at Sherborne.'

'And were they nasty to you – the boys?'

'No. I just didn't exist for them, that's all. One day, when I was about five, I wandered into one of the changing rooms, by accident. There was a lot of them there, naked, running in and out of the showers with their doings flopping about. No one tried to cover himself. They didn't mind if I saw,' said Brian, 'because I just didn't count. They didn't think, here's an innocent child, we ought to make ourselves decent and then send him about his business what he's got none of here, they thought (if they thought at all) here's nobody and never mind what nobody sees or makes of it.'

'Perhaps it only meant,' I said, 'that they accepted you like one of themselves . . . as part of the House, I mean.'

'As part of the fucking furniture,' said Brian; and forty-eight hours later he went to follow the drum.

Brian's hatred was so mindless, so utterly without concrete cause or any true insight into what goes on inside public schools, that it is not, in itself, of the faintest interest. What is of some interest is the dichotomy between Brian's loyalty to Cordwalles, its boys and its staff (he was anxious to please *him* and *her* to the very last, despite the meanness with which they were treating him) and his obsessive hatred of the schools which Cordwalles fed with boys and with which it was intimately connected.

Brian's accusation, that the Headmaster had behaved as feebly as he had done because he had been educated at a public school, was simply a pretext to discharge his fury (for fury it was, blind, quivering, obscene). His notion that boys at Sherborne didn't mind his seeing their *pudenda* because to them he was as nothing was just another pretext. But the fury itself was genuine: whence had it come and why?

I offer a conjectural answer.

Brian served faithfully under officers who were most of them from the type of school that he hated so much. As a Sergeant, he came to see *him* and *her* and those whom he still knew among the boys and staff at Cordwalles before he embarked for the Near East (the 'Middle East' as the War Office insisted on calling it, no doubt to make their task seem the more onerous) in 1941. I myself was no longer there, but I heard later that he was kindly received and took a proud farewell. He was later commissioned in the field and so privileged to eat and drink daily among old public school boys, all of whom, on the theory announced in his rage, should have been turned into 'spineless women' by their education. After the war he was given a regular commission in the Somerset Light Infantry, and so spent much of the rest of his life with them. He was treated, in the annual Cordwalles Old Boys' Letter, as an honorary ex-pupil of Cordwalles; and by some curious and ironical blunder was in one issue referred to as an old Sherbornian. I dare say that that was what he had always really wanted to be, and hence all the fuss in the first place.

I N THE SUMMER OF 1940 I was taken away from Cord-walles, not in disgrace, but because my parents considered the military area round Camberley to be a likely target for German bombers. I went without regret; several of my favourite masters (to say nothing of Brian) had gone off to fight, while two of my best friends had been removed for the same reason as I was. The only person I was really sorry to leave was Opie; but interesting as I had found his company and communications (and was to find them again later) he was somehow not the kind of fellow that inspired grief at parting. There was something prosaic about Opie that precluded tears, his own or another's. Placid Opie. Fat Opie. Shrewd Opie, who had seen through the education offered him at Haileybury, and wise Opie who had gone off to live among the trees. Opie (brave Opie) would stay in his cottage and teach at Cordwalles let the bombs drop thick as they might. In the end

[34]

none dropped at all, or not on Cordwalles, and I began to feel rather foolish about slinking away from the place; but at the time, as I say, I was not sorry to be gone. The feeling in the air in those early days of the war was all of movement, and it would have been invidious to be left static. (Later on one would pray for nothing else, but that is another story.)

So to Somerset I now came and was put to a new prep. school on the south shore of the Bristol Channel near an aerodrome in which my father was serving with the RAF. The school was a good one; unlike Cordwalles, it charged moderate fees, did not go in for dietary fads (simply kept us in a permanent and healthy state of hunger), won matches, taught Greek, won scholarships, and did not make clumsy boys do carpentry. Its Headmaster was called Captain Trent; he had been at Blundell's and King's College, Cambridge, and then, immediately afterwards, held a regular commission in the Army (Infantry of the Line) during the 1914 war. He would happily have gone freebooting off into this one had he not been prevented by his really rather awful (blue-stocking, Puritan, early Girtonian) wife, who insisted that it was his duty, as laid down by the Government, to stay and run the school. So he stayed, ran the school pretty well (though his wife was the one that coped with war-time shortages and regulations), and taught Association Football, history and geography . . . his lessons in the last two subjects consisting almost solely of the travel monologues and general memoirs of Captain Aloysius Trent.

'Agincourt,' he might say at the beginning of the lesson which was meant to be about it. 'Agincourt,' he would repeat, bouncing his bum experimentally on the only VIth-Form radiator and finally letting it settle on the only section that gave out any heat. 'It's really called "Azincourt", you know, in Picardy, quite near a place called Le Touquet, where my battalion was billeted for a month or so early in the last war. Le Touquet had been a swank French resort in peace time, and although it was all shut up now, there were still a few rich Frogs lurking in their villas in the sand-dunes.

'Some of these used to entertain us, and one day they got it into their heads that we'd like to drive over and have a picnic on the

[35]

field of Azincourt. Rather big of them, really, since that was where they were crushed to pieces by Henry V in whatever the year was, but I suppose they thought it would look good and help to promote goodwill in their guests and allies, et cet., et cet.

'So off we went one Sunday morning after Church Parade, in a De Dion Bouton or some juddering brute of a Frog motor, and a more scruffy and boring place than Azincourt you never did see. Just a flat, dull, damp field near a run-down farm. But as we were walking round this dismal field after what (I must admit) had been an Alpha Plus lunch – food and drink, you know, is what the Frogs do really well, and never mind their rotten revolution or boring old Rabelais – as we were plodding through the confounded mud, a young chap dressed as a French Lieutenant came up to us, and damn my soul if it wasn't Pierre de Malroy who had once spent a year with me under the same history master at Blundell's.

'This was because de Malroy's family had wanted him to learn English, had known people who lived near Blundell's in Tiverton, and had somehow got it into their heads that Blundell's was a really swish school – almost next to Eton – whereas in fact it is a middle class and provincial one of definitely the third rank. The Frogs always get that kind of thing wrong; they'd heard that one of the little princes had gone to a prep. school called Brudenell's and muddled the names up.

'Anyway, de Malroy had been with me at Blundell's, and now here he was at Azincourt (the guest of some Frog in a château round the corner). He had been taking an afternoon walk, he said, and "*heureusement*" had recognised me. All very touching, but I'd never had much time for the fellow (narrow forehead and blubber lips, not an agreeable combination) and what was I to do with him now?

'That, it turned out, was no problem at all,' said Aloysius Trent, shifting from ham to ham on the radiator and wrinkling his hockey stick nose. 'All I had to do – until my party was ready to go back to Le Touquet – was listen to de Malroy carrying on about the dear old days at Blundell's.

'Now, at this stage we'd better get something straight. Blun-

[36]

dell's was a jolly decent place in my day, and still is, as those of you that are going there will find out. What's more, Tiverton is a pleasant little town enough, and some of the countryside around there takes a lot of beating. But when you've said that, you've said the lot about Blundell's. It's rather like Magdalen College at Oxford – distinguished only, as some chappie once said, by its entire lack of distinction. I myself had a nice enough time there for five years, but most of the masters were pretty dim, and a lot of the boys had fathers in trade, and the world went by and knew not Blundell's; plenty of peace and quiet was the best you could say for it.

'And now here was this wretched fellow, de Malroy, squawking away like that old fool, Justice Shallow, in whatever part of *Henry IV* it is, all about what a great school Blundell's had been, and what daring fellows *we* had been, and what piping times we had enjoyed together. All a load of rubbish. I'd never been near him if I could help it and I'd certainly never enjoyed myself when I had been.

'Still, it was soon time to go back to Le Touquet, and that, one would have thought, was an end of de Malroy and all his balls about Blundell's. Only it wasn't. By some chance of the devil he was very soon after appointed interpreter or liaison officer or whatever to my battalion. Here's a go, I thought. But then who could have been more appropriate than de Malroy? He had uncommon good English – that at least had come out of his year at Blundell's. And of that English I had the benefit up and down and across the North of France for the next two months, always on the same ridiculous theme, the dashing days at grand old Blundell's and the swingeing times that he and I had had together.

'Which, as I've made pretty plain, we hadn't.' The hockey stick nose flexed itself from side to side (tick, tock, tick, tock). 'After a bit, it was clear to me that there was something *wrong* with Lieutenant de Malroy. I couldn't believe that his memory was all that defective – after all, it was only five years since we had both been at Blundell's. Either it was imagination or delusion or sheer invention. And whatever it was, why?

'I only found out on the day he was posted away from us.

[37]

Feeling delighted that my persecution was about to end, and feeling guilty because I was feeling delighted, I told my servant to help de Malroy's hump the blighter's kit to the wagon. Through the stupidity of all three of 'em, one of de Malroy's cases got left behind, standing all by itself as plain as a coffin on the improvised square on the Place in front of the Casino – we were back in Le Touquet again – while the wagon rumbled off towards Étaples. Very well, I said: it could be sent after him to-morrow; let it be taken to my quarters for to-night.

'And, as my servant brought it into my bedroom, the thing burst open . . . and out fell two score and more of books. English School Stories. Not Army pamphlets, or yellow novels, or *belles lettres*, or rude books with plain covers, or works of reference or mathematics, but Blackie's edition of public school yarns . . . with one or two higher grade novels of school life, I suppose you could call them, real literary stuff by pukka writers. Among these was one *very* curious job called *David Blaise*, by an old member of my college, E. F. Benson, which I remembered seeing in the library there but had never read before. *Quelle cochonnerie*, as the Frogs used to say. There was a scene in an open air squash court – they used to have 'em then – in which David Blaise's knickerbockers got so wet in the rain that they clung to his thighs, which started to show right through them – Leander pink – and excited the Head of his House. I ask you. Of course I may as well warn you now that you'll come across a lot of that sort of nonsense when you go to your public schools. The most sensible thing to do is to steer clear of it, or else some damn nosy parker will start making a lot of silly fuss. Where was I? David Blaise showing what he'd got in a squash court. Pretty high class performance, that book; even if he got a bit carried away about thighs, Benson was a clever cove and knew how to tell you a tale.

'And another good one was H. A. Vachell's novel, *The Hill*. All about Harrow. Romantic.' There was a crossing of thighs and a quiver of Captain Trent's dimpled chin. 'Two fellows go there at the same time and become friends and stay friends, until one of 'em is killed in the Boer War. At first they all think it's Scaife the

Demon that's died – the one that hit the ball clean over the Pavilion at Lord's in the Eton Match but was reputed to be "hairy at the heel". The telegram says "Demon dead died gloriously". But then a corrected version comes through saying "Desmond dead" et cet., Desmond being the hero's friend. Sentimental slush. Marvellous stuff. Had me crying like a baby the first time I read it. And those Harrow School Songs, quoted at the beginning of every chapter . . . "Forty Years On" – we all know that one. Here's another:

> "A quarter to seven and there goes the bell;
>   The rain is driving against the pane;
> But woe to the sluggard that turns again
>   And sleeps not wisely but all too well."

'Or what about this one:

> "You come here where your brothers came,
>   To the old school, long ago."

Gets you at the back of the throat, doesn't it?

'Anyway, there were these two splendid school stories in de Malroy's case, among many lesser ones. *Green of Grey House* – or was it *Grey of Green House*? And then that one – I can't remember its infernal name – in which a chap gets marooned on a bell-buoy. By the time the Navy gets to him he's stuck to it with the cold and they have to scrape him off with a Petty Officer's cutlass. Then there was *The Fifth Form at St. Dominic's* – with a damn fine cricket match that starts to turn crooked because the school bounder's got a large bet on it. Shane Leslie's *The Oppidan*. Damned silly man, Shane Leslie, at my college like Benson, but not a patch on EFB, just a nagging wind-bag, a fatuous bog-Irish bore. *Jeremy at Crale*, by Hugh Walpole: bold-faced boy with sensitive nature, or Mr Walpole having it both ways.

'Looking through them all, I noticed that de Malroy had thumbed certain passages absolutely yellow – practically sweated through the page in one case. And what all those passages had in

[39]

common was this: either they were the real tear-jerkers, like the scene in which the hero of *The Hill* realises that if he were asked to he'd lay down his life for his friend; *or* they were accounts of rattling adventures, generally shared between two friends, of the sort which de Malroy was constantly and untruthfully asserting that we two had shared at Blundell's.

'And so I realised more or less what must have happened. Before he came to England to go to Blundell's, he must have got hold of these kind of books and read them to prepare himself for the sort of life he was going to lead there. Where did he get 'em? God knows. But I once visited a château near Dieppe, and in the Nursery was a huge collection of Blackie's stories of girls' schools, perhaps an English Nanny had brought them over – but the point is that if there were Blackie's editions of *Hilda of Holmfield* and *Nancy Risks All* in a house in Dieppe, there can be no reason why there shouldn't have been copies of Blackie's books for boys in de Malroy's house in Rouen. So he read all about David Blaise and Desmond and Tom Brown (he was there too) and The Big Five and God knows who else, and he got himself all ready for a life full of thrills and spills and emotional school songs and Leander pink thighs and Forlorn Hopes on the rugger field – and he just didn't get it. Dear old, drab old Blundell's just did not put on that kind of a programme. As indeed he soon found out. But, whatever the reality, he still had a need for what he'd read about and what he'd hoped for. When he left, after his one year, he needed something to remember, for Christ's sake, something to tell his parents and his Frog chums (if he had any), something to share with other Old Blundellians should he meet them later . . . something which just had not happened to him. All that had happened to him was nothing. He wasn't even violently rejected or pointedly ignored. He had been treated with exemplary politeness, by myself as by others, pleasantly answered if he asked something, and also (so that he should not feel excluded) occasionally and amiably addressed. If he was not sought out, neither was he shunned. And simply on the strength of this, and, once again, on the strength of the contents of those books, he had built for himself a fictitious past in which he and I (or no doubt any other Old Blundellian he happened to meet) had taken part in mammoth rags, heroic protests, breath-taking alarums and excursions.

'Do you know,' said Captain Trent, 'I felt quite sorry for Pierre de Malroy. For the last two months I had avoided him whenever the uses of politeness allowed or the contingencies of the Service excused me, I had listened to his raptures with glazed eyes and neither applauded nor responded . . . and now he and his pathetic dream had gone, gone for good, snubbed, unloved, unheeded. God knew how long it would be before he met another Old Blundellian again and had another chance to relive in company, and not just in solitude, the great days and jolly days of school.

'So I would make it up to him, I told myself. First, I re-packed his books and secured his case, in such a manner that I hoped he would never realise that the contents had been disturbed; next I wrote him a note to accompany the case when it was sent on to him the next day. Remembering, not for the first time since our reunion at Azincourt, the case of the babbling and mendacious Justice Shallow ("Jesu, Jesu, the days that we have seen"), I said what a pleasure it had been to meet him and talk about old times, and concluded with Falstaff's kindly and conniving comment, "We have heard the chimes at midnight, Master Shallow." And so from then on,' ruminated Captain Trent, 'I suppose that his pitiful fantasies about Blundell's became more real and important to him than ever.'

SOMETHING ABOUT ALOYSIUS' account of *The Hill* caught my imagination. During the following holidays I saw a copy in a second-hand book shop. It was going for one shilling, which I did not possess. So great was my hankering that I carried it out under my overcoat – and was well punished during the next three weeks, not by moral guilt, but by fear of arrest. The book seller would have noticed my hanging about in that part of the shop, he would find *The Hill* gone, he would enquire for a ginger-haired boy of about thirteen in a black school overcoat and with a large pustule in the cleft of his chin, and presently there would come two men to knock on the door . . .

In the intervals of sweating with terror I managed to read *The Hill*. This, then, was Harrow at the turn of the century: what did I make of it?

Apart from the story of the two friends, which filled me with a 'pash', so to speak, on the pair of them, there seemed to me to be a number of interesting and (some of them) rather dubious propositions either stated or strongly implied by the text. Here are a few of the more outstanding.

1. (a) Harrow is a healthier school than Eton because it is on a hill, not in marshy ground by a river.

(b) Harrow is morally a healthier school than Eton because people who live on hills are hardy and simple-living, whereas people who live in valleys are lax if not Sybaritic.

From that day to this I have always imagined behaviour at Eton as corrupt and debauched, like Pompeii on its last day, and get a frisson of prurient pleasure whenever I go near the place. Equally, I have contrived to think of Harrovians as pure and clean-limbed, though I know from bitter experience that they can be masters, not indeed of whole-hearted wickedness (you have to look to Etonians for that), but of the squalid and petty con-trick, of the quick seduction of their best friend's sixteen-year-old daughter in the back of a taxi. It was not for nothing that the seedy anti-hero of Graham Greene's *England Made Me* used to wear an Old Harrovian tie to which he was not entitled – a mean and trivial piece of deceit worthy of a genuine Old Harrovian.

2. There is no liberty forbidden to a long-established servant (in this case, the House Butler) provided he is correct and deferential in his manner of address.

This was my first inkling of the basic joke in P. G. Wodehouse. I have always found it a pawky one.

3. Blood tells.

Although my own blood was indifferent at the best, I was prepared to go along with this item, as it seemed to me, on the evidence of *The Hill*, that 'good' blood quite as often told for bad marks (fatuous self-satisfaction and a concomitant propensity for missing the point) as for any possible merit.

4. It is better to have no money at all than to have made it in trade.

Obvious rubbish. My grandfather had made our family money by selling socks. Where should I be without it? Not sitting here comfortably (by this time my fear of arrest had subsided), eating black market choccies, warmed by black market coal, and reading a fascinating book about the sort of posh school which I myself was shortly to attend.

5. Good breeding is more important than cleverness.

Once again obvious rubbish, by the same token as proposition 4. However, if one fancied any sort of social career at one's public school, it might be that attention must be paid, even now in 1941, to these two crotchets of 1900. So I consulted one of my god-fathers, this one a goy called 'Uncle' Lionel Combes, who had himself been at Charterhouse whither I was bound the next autumn.

What rules, I comprehensively enquired, governed matters of conduct, class, brains and personal status in the school that had produced Judge Jeffreys, William Makepeace Thackeray, Lord Baden-Powell and General Dobbie of Malta?

Having very properly reminded me that he had been there from

1915 to 1919, and that all things change even in the most static institutions, 'Uncle Leo' began to deliver judgment.

'You have to remember' (Uncle Leo said) 'that Charterhouse was once a "City" school and has kept its city connections. For obvious reasons, then, it is attended by many sons of bankers, Hebrews and ship-owning Greeks for good measure. When you get that sort of a circus, you cannot expect that many of 'em will set breeding before cleverness or despise the money made in trade. Exactly the reverse. It is blood and breeding, particularly penurious blood and breeding, that will be despised, while money will always be admired, wherever it came from in the first place.

'My God, this beer is quite horrible. Please go to your father's best barrel this time.'

'It's locked up in his bedroom,' I explained. 'There's only the barrel in the kitchen.'

'Then I suppose that will have to do. What a mean hound your father is. But of course he went to Repton – tight fists clenched round midland brass.'

Having been furnished with another quart pot of porter from the barrel in the kitchen, Uncle Leo stretched full length on the camp bed on which he was spending the nights of his New Year's visit (RAF accommodation in war-time Yeovil was illiberal) and continued:

'Now, take racquets for example. A damn fine game, fast, exciting, graceful – and very, very expensive. The hard balls wreck the frames of the racquets; a proper player has to have a multiple press of three racquets or even five. You'd have thought that this – the sheer expense – would have been just the very thing to recommend the game to a purse-proud crew like the Carthusians I'm describing. Not a bit of it. It turned out that they were mean as well as rich. The war, you see, was an ideal excuse for not playing racquets: it was (they said) *unpatriotic* to use up all those balls, which had to be especially stitched by hand, and to break all those racquets, which had to be replaced, when the nation was so short of labour and materials.

'But the real reason they shunned racquets,' said my godfather, slopping beer on to his sheets, 'was certainly not patriotism, and not even meanness, but inverted snobbery. Here was an elegant and essentially upper class game (much played at Eton), and so they, the sons of banausic and mongrel rabble, were determined to despise it. It was stylish and beautiful and aristocratic and there-fore not for this spawn of the machine shops and the counting houses – and not for anyone else either, if they could help it. The spectacle enraged the middle class Philistines (which many of them were) and put to shame the money-minded scavengers (which many of the rest were); and bullies of both classes threatened and browbeat any younger or more civilised boy who looked like taking up the game. I was prevented from playing until I got my 1st XI Cricket Colours, which of course made me too grand a figure to be stopped – though even then I was much resented for "keeping racquet" at the school court. And I don't altogether wonder. You see, I only got my Cricket Colours (and so became powerful enough to please myself) through the most colossal fluke – a story from which there is much to be learnt.

'Cricket was hated by most of the type – a prominent type – which I've been talking about quite as much as racquets was . . . and for some of the same reasons : because it was stylish and tended to be associated (quite wrongly, as it happens) with the upper class, and also for one very different and very interesting reason : cricket took up a lot of space and time ; it was *leisurely* ; just the sort of thing to offend shekel-grubbing business chappies – all that time and effort and laboriously rolled green grass, and no one a penny richer at the end of it.* So cricket, although it was too big a thing to be altogether blackguarded like racquets, was in many quarters of Charterhouse despised and sneered at, and in minor ways sabotaged. *Everyone* had to play three times a week, you see, so there were a lot of rebels turned loose on to the field.'

Uncle Leo heaved himself up and waddled off for a pee that was audible through two closed doors.

'Now, at the beginning of my second last summer' (he resumed)

* N.B. My Uncle Leo was talking of 1918, not of 1986.

'I was still only what was called a 1st 'Tic (Peripatetic), which meant that I played for a pretty inferior sort of house team which contained no members of the 1st or 2nd XI. I used to bowl slow left arm, second change – not a star billing. But one afternoon it happened that our opponents, who were batting, were very anxious to get away early – there were some strawberries going in their house, it seemed, in honour of somebody's birthday, and it would be a case of first come, first served. So although the two or three proper cricketers insisted on batting properly and saw our opening and first change bowlers right off for the loss of only one wicket, the rebels then started to come in, knowing the strawberries would be served at 5.30 and scoffed by 5.31, and chucked their wickets straight down the drain . . . to my bowling. It wasn't difficult, you see, to prance down the wicket, miss one of my leg breaks on purpose, and get stumped. In the end,' said Uncle Leo with somewhat equivocal pride, 'I took 9 for 17.

'Meanwhile, the 1st XI leg break bowler had just been sacked for thieving. They were a wretched side, having a wretched season: so, "This fellow Combes," they said, "let's try him. Nobody's ever heard of him before, but 9 wickets out of 10 for 17 runs is a 1st 'Tic record, and though it was almost certainly sheer luck, who knows? There's certainly nothing to lose."

'So the next Wednesday there I was turning up on Green at 11.30 sharp for the match against the I Zingari . . . eleven stuck-up buggers if ever there were. The school went in first and after forty-five minutes of scraping and scrabbling were all out for sixty-three horrible runs (Combes run out nought) on the most beautiful wicket you ever did see. Typical weedy effort of a pox-awful side. As for the I Zingari, they were going around talking in hooty and haw-haw voices about how they'd probably drop this fixture next year, and meanwhile, "Let's get this pathetic thing over and go off somewhere decent for lunch."

'"All right", our captain said to me with a sad sigh, "so let's get it over, as they say, and get these snooty swine off the premises. You take second over from the school end. I only hope there's some glass left in Chapel when they've finished with you."

[46]

'Now my bowling' (Uncle Leo pursued) 'was left-arm round the wicket, slow leg breaks with an occasional Chinaman, mostly of a pretty low trajectory as I was too funky to toss them right up. Imagine my surprise, then, when my first ball seemed somehow to jerk loose from my hand much too early, then floated very high in the air and finally descended almost vertically on to the batman's bails while he was futilely flaying about underneath it.

'My next ball, instead of leaving my hand early, stuck to it until far too late, with the result that it hit the ground about a third of the way down the wicket and hopped on towards the batsman who struck at it with lordly contempt and utterly missed it, as many better players have done in just these circs ever since the game began at Hambledon. Combes: two wickets for no score in two balls.

'I did not get a hat-trick. My third ball was the only ball of a more or less decent length that I bowled during my entire spell; it was struck on to terrace and bounced clean through a stained glass window of the old Chapel – just what my captain had expected. But I very soon had revenge. My fourth ball was another balloon job, which the batsman tried to pull off his shoulders. He made a colossal yank at it, totally miscued, and delivered a dolly to mid-wicket. And so the thing went on. I had no control of the ball whatever, all my co-ordination was clean gone, and I sent down an unpredictable series of donkey drops, slow beamers, multi-bouncers and sneaks. The I Zingari, who had been swollen with overwhelming confidence before I bowled my first ball, were irritated beyond endurance by the time I had bowled my fourth. They had been conned out of three of their best wickets by a baggy-trousered clown whose flannels stopped four inches above the top of his socks; they suffered a total loss of morale and descended into the lowest depths of ineptness and humiliation.

'The match was indeed all over before lunch as our haughty opponents had proclaimed it would be, but it was we and not the I Zingari that had the right to chant "Non Nobis" and "Te Deum". For myself, I had taken 8 wickets for 13 runs; and my captain threw me his own pink cap, a token that I was being awarded my

1st XI Colours on the field itself, as the umpires gathered up the stumps.

'Of course a strict interpretation of the laws of cricket would have compelled both sides, since their first innings had been concluded so early, to go on and make a two innings match of it; but the paladins of the IZ were by now in such a rage that nobody thought to suggest this. Within ten minutes they were back in uniform (most of them were serving officers who had wangled a day off) and within twenty the last of them had departed by snarling Staff Car.

'And the explanation of my bizarre bowling? Very simple, when I came to think of it. The previous Sunday I had been visited by my mother and two sisters, who had clamoured to be taken on the river. My mother was a large lady and my sisters mountainous. The strain incurred by my arms and shoulders in rowing them up the Wye Valley nearly to Guildford and then back again to Godge had somehow disorganised certain muscles and ligaments used in bowling. As luck would have it, there had been no cricket between Sunday and Wednesday (rain on Monday and Corps on Tuesday), so that I had had no way of knowing, before Wednesday's match, how much my bowling had been affected by our river party – to which I had correctly attributed a slight stiffness of the upper arms without finding any cause here for worry. Had there been nets on Monday, as there would have been but for the weather, my condition would have been found out and my chance of glory denied me. As it was, a series of freak balls, totally unplanned by myself and not to be anticipated even by experienced batsmen, had undone the enemy, and a most unseemly David (I was bow-legged and obese, had no chest, far less than my share of neck, and three purple carbuncles with mauve stripes on what there was of it), an obscene dwarf of a David, had brought Goliath (eight Goliaths) to the dust.

'And so, having my cricket colours and being now a Major Blood, entitled to walk on the grass, furl my umbrella, stroll arm in arm with any other Blood I fancied (if any other Blood sufficiently fancied me), I was, as I told you earlier, much too big a man (in the figurative sense) to be told I couldn't play racquets . . . and I turned out, against all the odds and despite my lamentable figure, to be a very useful player, who was to be awarded "minor spos" [Minor Sports Colours] and play for the Second Pair the following autumn.'

A QUART OR TWO LATER, and after some rather boring accounts of his prowess as a racquets player, my Uncle Leo tapped a vein of fate and morality.

'But of course' (Uncle Leo proclaimed) 'life was not to be one long round of pleasure and success. Even in the summer the gods had already grown jealous of my triumph at cricket, and their agents here on earth were being briefed where to deploy the banana skins.

'The place and time chosen for my come-uppance was the annual Corps Camp on the Point-to-Point Course near Camberley in the first week of August.

'Now, you should know that my House Platoon was commanded by a horror called Plender-Greene, one of the most venomous enemies both of cricket and racquets (for the twisted social reasons I told you about earlier) in the entire school. Although he had no distinction in any other activity or department of the place, he was the Senior Under Officer in the Corps and wore officer's dress with a collar and tie and carried a sword on drill parades. As for me, with all my Major Bloodship, in the Corps I was Cadet Cunt. You are familiar with the term?'

'Well, Uncle Leo, Carson Parker in West Dorm said . . .'

'. . . And so Carson Parker in West Dorm was more or less correct, except that it is provided in place of, and not in addition to, the male penis or prick. So. I was Cadet Cunt, could do nothing right, had no interest in the Army (if no particular hatred

[49]

of it), had failed Cert A twice through sheer boredom, could not put on my puttees properly and had a tunic which exacerbated the carbuncles on my single inch of neck.

'Plender-Greene, on the other hand, was not only Senior Under Officer but had already been officially accepted (this, you understand, was the last summer of the war) as an aspirant for a commission in the Coldstream Guards. Since Carthusians had conspicuously not been in demand with the Brigade before 1915, and had been accepted then only because of an acute shortage of "officer material", this was rather a dubious honour. But Plender-Greene made a real production of it, strutting and preening round the race course, reminding everyone he met that he was off to the Brigade Squad as soon as camp was over and that he would be an Ensign in the Coldstream by Christmas. In fact the one fly in Plender-Greene's ointment was *me*: every time he looked at me, he was reminded that I was entitled to walk on the grass, furl my umbrella, and the rest, whereas he never had been and never would be. Even if he returned to Charterhouse with the rank of Field Marshal he *still* wouldn't be, as only returning Bloods, when we became Old Boys, enjoyed Bloods' privileges. Plender-Greene might be king at Camberley, but Cadet Cunt would always outrank him on social occasions at Charterhouse . . . simply because of *bloody cricket* . . . all of which made Plender-Greene as sick as shit.

'So Plender-Greene, appropriately enough, was the agent appointed by the gods to bring me low, to punish me for my pink cap and my elegant new press of three racquets (presented by my proud mother and sisters). His scheme of revenge was crude and injurious. In the middle of the race course, in those days, was a pond in which we were made to bathe – naked, as the custom then was, though I'm told prudish Headmasters are beginning to disapprove of that now. However, naked we bathed in my day, and a pretty disgusting sight we most of us were: if prudish Headmasters want to discourage lust, they'll allow the boys to continue to bathe naked, not make 'em cover up their beastly, hairy scrotums. But all that is by the way.

POWERFUL ST. JIM'S SERIES STARTS TO-DAY!

The GEM

THE BEST BOOK FOR BRITISH BOYS

2ᵈ

No. 1,367.   Vol. XLV.   EVERY WEDNESDAY.   Week Ending April 28th, 1934.

A DRAMATIC INCIDENT FROM "THE BOY WHO COULDN'T BE SACKED!"—WITHIN.

Levison roared and wriggled as Mr. Fitzgerald laid on the cricket stump, but he could not escape from the iron grasp of the cricket coach. He had looked for trouble and found it! The juniors had no sympathy to waste on the cad of the Fourth—they yelled with laughter.

Tom Merry & Co

"Gentlemen," said Tom Merry, "my suggestion is that we form——Oh!" Creak! Crash! There was a terrific rending as the woodshed roof gave way, and three flying forms came whirling down upon the meeting. The weight of Figgins & Co. had been too much for the roof!

Blake wrenched open the lid of the box, and four pairs of eyes gazed in astonishment at the contents. Gasps of utter dismay floated through Study No. 6. Instead of being full of tuck, the box contained earth, stones, and turf! "Figgins!" gasped Blake faintly. "That's where their feed came from!"

The swell of St. Jim's swung himself down the wall by his hands. Then he dropped, struck the earth with a sudden jar, and sat down. There was an ominous crunch—Arthur Augustus had sat on his own topper! "Bai Jove! I've fallen on somethin'!" he gasped.

Father and Son

Thomas Arnold

Matthew Arnold

In Disgrace

Youth on the prow, pleasure at the helm. The fourth of June at Eton

Eton School Yard

A boy's study

Eros with cricket bat

'Plender-Greene's plan was to have my clothes removed while I was bathing and leave me stranded, a good quarter of a mile from our own lines; and not simply that: this was to occur on the last morning bathe of the camp, just before we all marched, in full Field Service Marching Order, to Camberley Station, where we would take a train back to Charterhouse, there to stack away our tents and equipment and disperse for the summer holidays. If only I could be delayed long enough at the pond, it would be too late for me to reach the Charterhouse lines – even if I could bear the embarrassment of crossing the course naked and passing through a field unit of the Veterinary Corps – before the Carthusian contingent had marched off, tents struck, drums beating, complete with the last pot and pan in the horse-wagons, leaving me totally desolate and resourceless, the Ariadne of Camberley Heath.

'Plender-Greene's chief problem, then, was how to keep me in the pond long enough. He chose the classic method: temptation to dalliance. If he could find someone to dally with me, he reasoned, then I, that was too hideous to get much – to get any – dalliance in the normal course, would surely be only too pleased to dally back. In the event, he managed to bribe the House Tart, a much coveted blond of fourteen, to take on the job. In return for two pounds (a huge sum in those days) the blond undertook to keep me frotting in the pond and the nearby bushes until the school Fifes and Drums struck up with the "British Grenadiers", this being the sign that the Column was moving off. The blond would then put on his own uniform and head by himself for the station, his absence in the line of march being condoned, and my own concealed, by Senior Under Officer Plender-Greene, who would also arrange for the blond's heavy kit to be carried to Camberley for him in one of the wagons.

'By the way' (asked Uncle Leo) 'You *do* understand what means the blond would employ, and what was supposed to be the attraction?'

'Yes, Uncle Leo. Carson Parker in the West Dorm . . .'

'. . . So, one way and the other, our man Carson Parker is a bit inaccurate. As I hope I have made clear, it is *not* a matter of inciting each other to pee. However, in broad terms you seem to understand the thing.

'Now, what the blond didn't know' (continued Uncle Leo) 'was that Plender-Greene, as it subsequently turned out, was planning to do the dirty on him and steal *his* clothes too. Apparently one of Plender-Greene's cronies had once heard the blond describe Plender-Greene as "common" because he lived in Purley. (The blond lived in Sunningdale, by Carthusian standards of money-snobbery a very acceptable place.) By stranding the blond as well as me, Plender-Greene would get another helping of revenge of an even more appetising flavour; for whereas to be stranded nude by oneself may be counted by the world as no more than a misfortune, to be stranded nude with a piquant companion exposes both oneself and him to dangerous and even criminal charges.

'So that's what the House Tart didn't know – that Plender-Greene was pulling the plug on him. But there was also something that Plender-Greene didn't know: ever since the age of eight and a game of hot cockles with a great uncle, I had cared only for old men – fat, fruity old men – who were of course only too happy to get off with a number as young as me, being too old and desperate to mind my ghastly figure or striped carbuncles. So I was very well provided on the sexual front: not only did I not need Plender-Green's luscious blond bait, not only would I not be attracted by a boy of his age, I should be positively revolted – all that loathsome smooth flesh when all I longed for was layers of crinkled blubber.

'More beer, please, my boy. It's begining to taste a lot better . . .

'. . . And so,' (my Uncle Leo said) 'when, as our comrades began to drift away back to our lines, the blond started splashing me and leering, I was absolutely indifferent.

' "Keep yourself to yourself, young Randal," I said.

'He tried a few teasing poses and even played with himself a bit under the water, but this was getting him nowhere, and so he had the sense to realise. He decided to abandon his mission (or so I now reckon with benefit of hindsight) and went for his clothes, presumably intending to make his way to the station alone, as planned, and there to try to convince Plender-Greene that he had done his best to detain me and deserved the second sovereign (the first having been paid in advance). I too left the pond and went to where my clothes should have been . . . at some distance from Randal's. Neither of us found them. At first I thought I had mistaken the place and hunted around; Randal, on the other hand, being privy to the plot, at once realised roughly what had happened.

'"That pig Plender-Greene," he called to me: "I always said he was common."

'"What's Plender-Greene got to do with it?"

'In ten seconds flat he told me: a sharp child, that Randal.

'"What are we going to do?" I said.

'"*You* are going to 'save' me from drowning, then run to that Veterinary unit for assistance. No one will mind you being nude in the circs. You'll need help with me here, you tell them, and somebody to go up to the Charterhouse lines and explain what's happened to us before they set off for the station. And don't go and get a rise while you're saving me," he said, forgetting my recent chaste behaviour, and vanished beneath the surface.

'So Randal "nearly drowned" and I "saved" him, without getting a rise, and was heartily acclaimed for my presence of mind and bravery. In the general excitement no one worried about our clothes; we were carried away on stretchers, wrapped in blankets. Plender-Greene, seeing his game was up, restored our uniforms to us, pretending to everyone else that he had collected them from the bank of the pond, was falsely accused by Randal of trying to touch him up under the blankets when he brought the uniforms to the Red Cross Tent (which had been struck but was re-erected in our honour), was instantly expelled (although he had left Charterhouse, he was still under school discipline for the duration of the Camp), and never even sniffed a commission in the Coldstream or anything else. Why the gods decided to switch from his side to mine at the last minute, I shall never know: perhaps one of them was keen on Randal and didn't like the way in which Plender-Greene was chizzing him.'

[53]

'But Uncle Leo . . . did all this really happen?'

'Pretty well, though I've dramatised a bit and made it neater. In real life these things tend to ramble on; so I've tried to give it some shape. But true in the main it is. Surely you must realise that somebody who admits that he is attracted to old men is unlikely to be a liar? Liars always end up by presenting themselves favourably, whatever admissions of petty faults they make along the line. Myself, as you notice, has not had a single good thing to say of myself. My cricket was a grotesque fluke, I've told you, and when the crisis came at the pond, Randal – three years and a half younger – had to do all the thinking and give the orders. Not a word of praise have I said for poor Lionel.'

'You did say you turned out quite decent at racquets.'

'Until I got a hit in the face in a doubles match and gave it up for squash out of funk.'

'How did you get on at cricket . . . after your big match?'

'For the rest of that summer quarter I just scraped by. Our Captain guessed more or less what had happened, you see, and didn't often put me on to bowl. He thought it was a joke – he was that kind of fellow. But he warned me he wouldn't be able to carry me like that for the following season, when he would still be there . . . so we made a little plan. I shammed an injury to my back in the Easter hols, but because I was a Colour I was allowed to go away with the XI for all matches – as "supernumerary scorer". My Captain enjoyed arranging that, to spite the anti-cricket brigade. In the end' (mused Uncle Leo) 'most things at Charterhouse were arranged in order to spite someone else, or to do somebody down. The City approach, you see, as I said to you earlier: grown men in the City demonstrate their success by getting best of one another about cash; their sons at Charterhouse demonstrate their success – or did in my day – by getting best of one another about face. Those are the snobberies of Charterhouse: cash and face. As for breeding, intellect, merit, talent – "No Sale," the Register rings up, "No Sale, No Sale."'

A T LAST I was at my public school.
Some eight months after my conversation with Uncle Leo, I had arrived at Charterhouse. Now the actual world of the Public School, no longer reported by mouth or print, but made physically concrete in three dimensions of space and mentally palpable in three others of scholarship, morality and custom, was to come directly under my eyes.

As a Junior Scholar, I sat, for my first quarter, in the Remove, under Charles Timon ('Bushy') Blake, an old Wykehamist with a trowel beard, flaring eyebrows and a staggering size in black boots. Bushy clearly shared Uncle Leo's low opinion of the kind of pupils that came to Charterhouse (money-grubbing and heedless of quality, whether personal or intellectual) and felt it his duty to preach the gospel of Winchester, high-minded and unworldly, without fear, favour or exception.

The first vehicle he used for the purpose was the life and character of Savonarola, the puritan preacher of Florence. It will be remembered that Savonarola felt called upon to excoriate the Florentines, not only for their addiction to bodily pleasure but also for their love of literature and the arts. He invited them to make a bonfire of their fripperies, pagan verses and vain artefacts, from scent phials to Sandro Botticellis. This they did, but, overcome by revulsion while it was burning, threw Savonarola on top of it. And serve him right.

This was the rather compressed version of Savonarola's career that I served up to Bushy in my first weekly history test, and I was at once called sternly to account.

Bushy's first charge was that I had taken a frivolous and light-minded tone over a grave matter – religion.

His second (quintessentially Wykehamist) was that I had not tried to understand the fundamental issues involved. Savonarola's crusade against material pleasure, he said, was entirely praiseworthy: he was acting out the spirit and letter of the Ten Commandments and obeying the word of the Lord God whom he served. As for his hostility to the arts, this was based on his conviction that the ornamentation of private houses and churches, like the orna-

[55]

mentation of the body, led to an interest in aesthetic and sensuous matters that might not necessarily be sinful in itself but was quite definitely sinful – indeed abominable – when it became an indulgence that distracted the mind and the soul from worship and adoration of the Deity. We went to church to entreat forgiveness and to vow amendment, not to admire altar pieces and murals. While at home, we were meant to nourish and recruit our minds and bodies in preparation for the whole-hearted performance of whatever services might be required of us by God; we were not intended to spend our time in idolatrous enjoyment of paintings, statues and tapestries, any more than we were intended to pamper our palates and gorge our pancreas with luxurious culinary confection.

Bushy's third charge (also *echt* Wykehamist) was that I had sneered at a man ('and serve him right') who had died in the discharge of his intellectual, moral and spiritual duty.

He then marked me with nought out of 25.

This dismal score drew upon me the attention of the Headmaster, Robert Birley. In his capacity of house-master of my House, he had been perusing the fortnightly marks of members of the House, with a view to summoning the more notable cases for praise or censure. When I entered his study, I expected the latter; but I had reckoned without one thing: Robert Birley was not an Old Wykehamist, like Bushy, but an Old Rugbeian, and as such was less theoretical and never wholly absolute in his judgments, always allowing that, however correct a verdict might be in logic or morality, it could nevertheless be liable, *in human practice*, to qualification or even reversal. The Rugbeian tradition, after all, is based on the combined utterance of the two Arnolds: a body of law laid down by Thomas but interpreted, re-cast, and rationally or humanely – sometimes even humorously – contradicted by Matthew. What I now received, therefore, from Rugbeian Robert, was not instant rebuke but a request for an explanation.

I explained. It seemed to me, I said, that there was a fundamental difference in the matter between myself and Bu – and Mr Blake; and while I made no claim at all to be his equal in understanding, I could not think I had the Savonarola affair as calamitously wrong as his marking of my paper would suggest.

'Savonarola was an unattractive character,' said Robert the lover of the arts and frequent reader of Matthew Arnold, 'but we have to remember that his concern was with a matter infinitely more important than the arts: he was concerned with the four last things, with death, judgment, heaven and hell, with the fate of our immortal souls,' said Robert the man of God and the occasional reader of Matthew's father, Thomas. 'In any case,' said Robert, 'what Mr Blake was really doing was punishing you for bad manners and conceit, for setting yourself up as an authority qualified to pronounce on matters well beyond your years, and for being flippant about the painful death of a man of great physical and spiritual courage. How would *you* like to have faced up to a mass of art-besotted Florentines and told them that they must burn their treasures to be saved? But this said,' said Robert the hater of Philistines, 'I must agree that you have a point. Can you imagine it, making a bonfire of the beautiful and the irreplaceable? Madness – and that of course is the probable explanation. Savonarola was a fanatic so fanatical that he probably welcomed his own martyrdom. So in a sense "Serve him right" is a correct and not uncharitable epitaph, though not in the way you obviously meant it. Anyhow,' concluded Robert the man of moderation and the man I came to love, 'you will have learnt from all of this not to be pert, least of all when sitting under Mr Blake.'

B USHY BLAKE'S next excursion into Wykehamist diatribe placed him in a rather more sympathetic light, though he was still much wrapped around in the cloud and fire of Sinai.

The Greek text he had chosen for us in our first quarter was

Xenophon's *Anabasis*, or Retreat of the Ten Thousand, which tells how Xenophon, as the elected general of an Expedition hostile to the interests of his own city of Athens, led his men from the heart of Asia Minor (where they had all been cut off) through hundreds of leagues of strange and cruel country back to the Mediterranean Coast. The great moment – and it is a great moment – comes when the Army reaches a crest and

'Θάλαττα, Θάλαττα,' they shout: 'the sea, the sea.'

At this stage Bushy quite simply ended our construe for the day (anything that followed could only have been an anti-climax) and launched into an exegesis.

He began by reminding us that Xenophon and his Army had been in Asia Minor with questionable if not treasonable intent. This raised the enquiry (eminently Wykehamist) how far it was permissible to admire courage when it was exhibited in a dubious or unethical cause or pursuit.

'Now, Xenophon was more than merely courageous,' Bushy conceded. 'He was, for a start, loyal to his troops. He could easily have fled by himself and got clear –

"Down to Gehenna or up to the Throne
He travels the fastest that travels alone" –

Rudyard Kipling. But he stayed and suffered with his men. He showed great intelligence, resource, endurance and restraint. He bore – and he forbore, for although many of his soldiers were stupid, mutinous, negligent or despairing, he managed to keep them together and coax them over desert and mountain to the sea.

'He crowned it all by writing a matchless account of the campaign, which has given pleasure and instruction for many centuries. And yet,' said Bushy, 'this whole affair is tainted by its origin in treacherous self-seeking. It is impermissible [a common Wykehamist word] simply to detach the episode of the retreat and pronounce that, taken by itself, it exemplifies all the noblest qualities of mankind, when we know very well that the occasion of the retreat was the well-merited result of lies, treachery and

[58]

ambition. Nor is Xenophon exonerated by the fact that he took over as Commander-in-Chief only at the time when the retreat began. He had been a party to the launching and the crooked purpose of the expedition from the very beginning. He cannot be excused his wickedness on account of his heroism. But can he be forgiven it?

'At first there may seem a strong case for forgiveness or pardon. His achievement, one is tempted to say, surely nullifies his crime. But does it?

'When I was a small boy at my 'totheran [Carthusian slang for prep. school, adopted by Wykehamist Bushy in kindly condescension] we had a system of stars for good work or actions, of bad marks for idle or contumelious conduct, and of stripes for flagrant delinquency. One bad mark was cancelled by one star. One stripe equalled three bad marks. The account was raised weekly.

'One week I had two stripes and seven stars, which left one star in credit. On handing them in on Saturday, I was informed that as punishment for the two stripes I should be barred from the lecture arranged for that evening and sent up to bed instead. The lecture, with lantern slides, was to be on The British System of Canals, an entertainment that may appear to you somewhat prosaic; but in those days, when a lantern was still a *magic* lantern, when treats of any kind were almost as rare as the Greek Calends, we hungered for such lectures.

'So I pleaded that my seven stars cancelled my two stripes. Was not a bad mark cancelled by a star? Then surely two stripes, which equalled six bad marks, must be cancelled (and rather more) by seven stars?

'One bad mark, I was told by the Headmaster (a Wykehamist, as I myself was later to become), was trivial; *de minimis non curat lex*. But two stripes, or six bad marks, all incurred within one week, indicated an almost violent decline in conduct and put the whole matter on a different level – a level not far removed from evil itself. Evil could not be cancelled out or excused by achievement, least of all by mere academic achievement, by mere cleverness, as

[59]

was mine. It could be *forgiven*, but only after it had been *punished*. Therefore I would miss the delectable lecture – and be forgiven.

'So it is, if I may compare my small things with others very great, in the whole matter of Xenophon, his good deeds (his magnificent deeds) and his evil or wickedness. The former cannot cancel the latter out, but the latter may be forgiven once it has been punished. In some circumstances the achievement itself may be said to constitute a punishment: for, although nothing will be forgiven on account of "cleverness" (as my Headmaster had it) or talent or even the conscientious use of intelligence, there can be forgiveness if the achievement necessitated strong elements of suffering, anxiety or grief.

'And so we ask ourselves, did Xenophon suffer enough, on the road from the heart of darkness to the sea, to be forgiven his earlier treachery? And the answer must be that God and His Son are the only auditors of that account.'

B Y THE FOLLOWING SUMMER I had begun to attend the lessons in English Literature given by the Master of the Sixth Form, A. L. ('Uncle') Irvine, another old Wykehamist, true enough to the mould but of a distinctly wider bore or calibre than Bushy Blake.

'The Uncle' had a globular trunk surmounted by a bald, globular head. He swore by the 'Three "C"s' (Classics, Cricket and Christianity – probably in that order). As well as being a genuine, though never top-class, Scholar of Latin and Greek, he had a deep and wide affection for all English Literature, a detailed knowledge of Nineteenth-Century Fiction and Verse, and also a general knowledge of European Art which enabled him to give an outstanding series of weekly Art Lectures that lasted through the entire Oration and Long Quarters (i.e. the Michaelmas and Easter Terms). He was a man of accomplishments: a very fair cricketer and a steady lawn tennis player, he was always ready for a game of Eton Fives, had a cunning hand with an *épée*, possessed an agreeable singing voice, botanised and bird-watched companionably, and played a passable game of Chess (Backgammon too, but refused to play the latter for a stake). All this he managed at the age of well over sixty when he would certainly have been retired had it not been for the war. The younger men went off to fight, while the Uncle (twice the man that any of them were) returned to Charterhouse to teach. One blessing at least the war had bestowed on us: the Uncle.

The English Lessons at which I first made his acquaintance were remarkable for three things: the rare pleasure with which he endowed the subject; the gusto with which he read selected passages (he did a tremendous turn with the death of Georgie Osborne at Waterloo, and a succulent take-off of the carnal Bishop ordering his Tomb at St Praxed's); and the Uncle's laughter, deep and unquenchable as that of Homer's gods. Jesu, how the old man could laugh: almost anything could set it off: an unintentional pun, an error in taste, a spoonerism, a howler, a false quantity, a clumsy rhyme – and back went the bald, round head and up and out came the gurgling merriment, ascending through the Sixth Form ceiling to the sky itself.

'I am sometimes afraid,' said a friend, 'that one day when the Uncle is laughing he will have a seizure.'

'Not a bad way to go,' another friend said.

The first time I heard the Uncle laugh was in the February of 1942, warming us all in the bitter war-time winter. At this period I was on the edge of a series of personal, academic and athletic triumphs, and did not need as much warming as many others; but still I felt the cheering current and was thankful. Later, when the Uncle's bursts of jocosity heralded the spring and then woke the drowsy afternoons of summer, my triumphs were complete. Undisputed first of the Remove, a leading junior cricketer, popular with my seniors and by some of them much admired, I was the *nonpareil* and knew it. I became flighty, capricious, opinionated, vain. This showed in my work, both for Bushy and the Uncle.

[61]

But, whereas Bushy was the pious and cloistered type of Old Wykehamist, the Uncle was of the worldly and bustling sort, who got around the place and made it his business to know a great many things about one apart from the state of one's work. While the Uncle's morality was strict, his intelligence was versatile and tolerant; he had a curious mind; like Odysseus, he had had himself bound to the mast (so to speak) so that he might listen but not succumb to the Sirens' Song.

One afternoon in June I met by chance with the Uncle, who was riding his bicycle. On seeing me he dismounted.

'I'm going to watch the 1st XI on Green,' he said. 'Like to come?'

'Very much, sir,' I said, and meant it.

So the Uncle wheeled his 'grid', refusing to let me take it for him, and talked of the trees, while I walked at his side, waiting for a chance to be clever.

'The old writers say,' said the Uncle, 'that each tree has its nymph or dryad, who lives for 999 years. When she comes to this age, both she and her tree die.'

'Suppose the tree dies earlier, sir?'

'A nice question. After all, most do. Some say the nymphs wander, at first forlorn and bereaved, but later getting up to trouble.'

Here was my chance.

'Menopausal outbursts?' I said.

'There is an empty seat here,' said the Uncle, ignoring my remark. 'They tell me,' he said as we sat down, 'that you are having a very exciting and successful summer.'

I smirked.

'I've been lucky, sir,' I said, meaning, 'I'm the *most*.'

'An agreeably modest attitude,' said the Uncle, seeing right through it, 'of a kind often difficult to sustain. I remember a contemporary of mine at my 'totheran – Mark Jolliffe, he was called – who signally failed to do so. We had been fond of one another and kept in touch for many years after we left this 'totheran of ours. He too had a lot of luck . . . until he started taking the credit for it. You see what I mean?'

'Yes, sir,' I said, truthfully and defensively.

'Shrewsbury he was at,' the Uncle said. 'Head of the School, Captain of Cricket and just about everything else. He even held a Commission as Cornet in the Yeomanry.'

'While he was still at Shrewsbury, sir?'

'In those days you could, you know. Something to do with being a senior member of the school Corps, which was part of the Auxiliary Forces. Something like that. All that kind of thing was on a much looser basis then. We're going back to before the Boer War, do you see? That man Carter,' he said, naming a prominent member of the XI, 'bats like an ape. Just look at him. He ought to be in a menagerie.'

'What a splendid ring it has,' I said, still thinking (as I was meant to be) of Mark Jolliffe. 'The word Cornet.'

'Latin *cornu*, a horn. In Roman times the standard bearer carried a horn, and probably blew it, instead of a banner. Mark, of course, carried nothing. But he was pardonably proud of his spurs and tight trousers – he had a good leg, I remember – and the chain mail he wore on his shoulders.'

A Cornet of Yeomanry, I thought: one in the eye for Uncle Leo's Under Officer Plender-Greene.

'But the trouble was' (said the Uncle) 'that Mark's commission in the Yeomanry was *very* temporary, valid for as long as he stayed at Shrewsbury and not a day longer. His great ambition was to get another commission of the same kind, but a much *steadier* one. Not a Regular Commission – he didn't want that – but something in the Reserve, which he could boast about while he was at Oxford, where he had won a Scholarship to Brasenose. He was going to take this up the following autumn, and he thought it would be amusing to parade about the place in Mess Kit now and again – being too ignorant to realise that officers never wore uniform except in the field, in barracks or in camp. He knew reservists dined in Mess Dress, but he didn't know that they did this only when they were with the Colours. Apart from anything else, Mark was rather lazy; he never bothered to go into things properly – to *find out*.'

[63]

So Mark Jolliffe, the Uncle told me, had decided to apply to the King's Shropshire Light Infantry (formerly the 53rd of Foot) to see if they could fix him up with a commission in the Militia or the Reserve. The KSLI depot was at Copthorne Barracks, within ten minutes' walk, the school and the regiment had always been close, many of the officers of the KSLI were Old Salopians and had their boys at the school, there was an annual cricket match on the school ground and an annual dinner in the Depot Mess. The KSLI could arrange it all for him, thought Mark Jolliffe: just the job.

So the thing was set in train. The Commanding Officer of the Shrewsbury School OTS put Mark's name forward. Mark underwent some infantile test or exam. He then went to dine in the Mess in the Depot, and was found to be a pretty acceptable fellow. Some said it was a pity he wasn't putting in to be a Regular. It was all fixed, in short, bar the final formalities (something to do with the Army Council or the War Office), and Mark had already warned his father's tailor in London that he would be in to be measured for his KSLI Mess Dress on the first day of the holidays. In the circs, then, he was much looking forward to the termly visit of the Depot Officers to Shrewsbury School, an occasion on which they were accustomed to make a perfunctory routine inspection, automatically award a high commendation (to be notified to the local General Officer Commanding), eat a huge cold lunch, and later examine some of the younger boys for Certificate 'A' – or whatever the equivalent then was.

'I'm questioning them in tactics,' said a mauve-faced Captain who sat next to Mark at the luncheon, 'which means that I just get 'em to chatter away about this and that, and then see whether I think they'd be the right sort of chaps for the regiment later on. Would their faces fit in the Mess, I ask myself. If they would, then I give 'em 8 out of 10 for tactics and suggest they should think of joining us one of these days.'

'Ha, ha,' went Mark, genuinely amused.

'By the way,' said the Captain, 'we're all delighted you're coming on to our roll as a reservist. See you at camp in August, I hope?'

'Wouldn't miss it for the world,' said Mark, making a mental note to add two sets of Service Dress to his order with his father's tailor.

'Righty-hoh,' said the Captain as the party reluctantly rose: 'off for an afternoon's tactics.'

The fifth or sixth boy that the Captain examined in tactics was called Millington. He was a nice, fresh, brown boy, who looked the Captain straight in the eye when he saluted him and did not flop about when told to stand easy.

'Which House are you in?' asked the Captain.

Millington told him.

'Ah,' said the Captain, 'Mark Jolliffe's House. But I don't suppose that you see much of *him*.'

'I'm his study fag, sir,' said Millington.

'Does he give you a rough time, ha, ha?' the Captain said.

'He is exceedingly kind, sir . . . provided one is prepared to listen to him.'

'Rather a privilege for a boy of your age. What does he talk about? Cricket? Oxford? The Regiment?'

'Himself, sir,' Millington said.

'Most of us do,' said the Captain, beginning to be uneasy.

'Certainly, sir. And very interesting Jolliffe is about himself.'

'In what way?'

'He likes to tell you how clever he's been.'

'Look here,' said the Captain, being now very uneasy indeed, 'who's side are you on?'

'On Jolliffe's, naturally, sir. He's a very considerate fag-master, and he tips well. And these stories about how clever he's been are often very funny. Would you like to hear one?'

'I suppose so.'

'Well, sir, he's going up to Brasenose next term. As he's got a scholarship, he wants to make quite sure that the fellows there don't think he's just a muff or a swot, and so he's arranging to impress them with being an officer on the reserve. He'll wear the uniform sometimes.'

'He'll *what*?'

[65]

'Wear the uniform, sir, in the evenings. At dinner parties and so on.'

'He told you this?'

'Oh yes, sir. He was so pleased with the way he'd arranged it all, you see. "What I'd really like," he said, "is to stay in the Yeomanry. Tight trousers and spurs, and proper county people, not just middle class imitations. But they won't let me do that once I'm finished with the Corps here, because it's the wrong sort of commission; so I'm fixing up to join those frumps at Copthorne. Provincial as gaiters and dowdy as mutton, with a uniform as dull as mud, but a fellow must go somewhere, and they're certainly very convenient. I had dinner with them all the other night and sucked up no end, admiring their boring cases of medals and playing stupid rough games after dinner.'

'I thought you said you were on Jolliffe's side?'

'I am, sir. I agree with every word he says.'

'I think, Millington, that you'd better fall out.'

'As you say, sir.'

How much of what Millington reported had actually been said to him by Jolliffe no one ever really knew, but of course Jolliffe's effort to procure himself a reserve commission in that quarter – or almost any other – was dished for ever. But why had Millington let Jolliffe down in this appalling fashion? If Jolliffe, as he said, was a kindly and open-handed fag-master, why should Millington make such treacherous use of what Jolliffe had told him in confidence?

'It appeared later,' said the Uncle as we sat on the bench on Green,' 'that Mark, like many fellows going through a heady patch, had over-reached himself. If you have a confidant, it is unwise to annoy him. Now, Millington's father was a highly placed official in the Bank of England. Mark, conceiving in his conceit that his lightest thoughts were worth broadcasting and that everyone coveted his golden banter, always referred to Millington senior as "the Cashier". Despite Millington's quiet insistence that his father was an expert economic adviser at ministerial level, "How's the Cashier?" Mark would say when

[66]

Millington had a letter or saw his parents at a week-end: "spotted any stumers lately?"

'And so it was that Millington, goaded for too long in a sensitive area, which Jolliffe had been too blind or self-infatuated to perceive, wounded by the cheap insult to the father he loved and admired – that Millington, I say, saw his chance and took his revenge. Jolliffe, you see, had gone too far. It is said that he profited by this lesson, Raven, and took care never again to be dominated by ἄτη, which is the Greek for extravagance of mind leading to loss of judgment, or ὕβρις, which means the brand of insolence that causes a man to forget that others, too, have their feelings and their pride.'

O F COURSE I ignored the Uncle's kind and tactful advice. At that age one was bound to. I over-reached myself all right: I welcomed ἄτη with open arms, nursed ὕβρις in my bosom, and came, as I deserved to, a real cropper. By the time I was fifteen and a half, a year or so after the Uncle told me his admonitory tale, I had become disillusioned, sullen, unwashed and foul-mouthed, one of the least popular boys in my house, a total failure in my second summer's cricket, covered with pimples and seldom sought out even by those in the last extremities of sexual deprivation. That my school work still prospered, and that I gradually recovered my confidence in other regions, and with it my physical appeal, my more amiable habits, and so my popularity as well, I owe largely to one man.

Vincent (Peter or 'Sniffy') Russell was an exquisite pianist and a fastidious composer of Latin Verses. He had other attributes (he was a passable actor, a sympathetic house-master, a dedicated if volatile teacher of ancient philosophy) but what I principally remember of him is the pianist and the Latin poet.

I came to his notice, when at the nadir of my public and personal fortunes, because I was the only boy in his Greek set who seemed to understand Plato's dialogue, *The Meno*. This is a particularly silly work, during which Socrates takes a slave boy step by step through an elementary and common-sense geometrical proof and then claims that, since the boy has understood the proof without any previous instruction in geometry, he must in truth have 'remembered' the theorem from a former existence in the world of mathematical ideas, and must therefore have an immortal soul. Nonsense, of course. But the dialogue has two merits: it is written in the sweetest Attic; and it is so lucidly presented that a sensitive reader must find it ungrateful, indeed almost barbarian, to expose the obvious logical flaw. In one word, it has charm. Peter Russell and I appreciated the charm and the rest of the set did not, so we became allies. Recalcitrant, boorish, repulsive as I then was, he took me under his wing and cherished me . . . whereupon things started to come right.

Peter Russell had been at Cheltenham, a sprawling school in the town of that name. I never heard him talk of it except in one connection: Maurice Bowra, the prolix scholar and loud-mouthed Warden of Wadham College, Oxford, who had also been at Cheltenham. Bowra was Peter's hero. 'The only old pupil from Cheltenham with any distinction at all,' he used to say, 'a true Renaissance man. Scholar, soldier, poet . . .'

'Soldier?' I said.

'First world war. He used to tell the story of the Officer Cadet in his squad at OTS who broke wind on parade. The fellow took two smart steps backward (being in the rear rank), farted like something out of Rabelais, then took two steps forward to rejoin his rank. He was instantly placed in close arrest, but was able to point in his defence to a section in an eighteenth-century manual of drill – a section that had never been rescinded and prescribed the precise action, in case of needing to fart, that Bowra's chum had taken. The authorities said that that was a drill for private men; officers or aspirant officers, they said, should never fart on parade however badly they might want to. Bowra then "discovered" a

[68]

passage which he claimed had been in the first edition of Captain Gronow's Memoirs but had been excised from all subsequent editions and therefore was not as well known as it should have been:

'"Axminster told me that on one occasion he was riding just behind His Grace [Wellington], when my Lord Duke lifted his rump from the saddle and delivered a swingeing f-rt. Axminster himself was upwind of His Grace but General Sir James Mertens, who was in the lee of him, was somewhat embarrassed.

'"'What's the matter, Mertens,' says his Grace: 'never heard a f-rt before?'

'"'Aye, Duke,' said Mertens, who for all his daintiness was a man of mettle, 'and smelt one too, from a tosspot in Vauxhall Gardens. His doxy bade him be off to the jakes before he followed it up with a t-rd.'

'"'Never,' said Axminster to me, 'did I see my Lord Duke so put out.'"

'Bowra had wished to produce this fabricated but typically zestful passage (typical, that is both of his own zest and Gronow's) as evidence for the defence, on the ground that if Field Marshals and Commanders-in-Chief could fart on parade, so could Officer Cadets. But, before the case came to trial, it was quashed on the order of the Commandant, who knew the offending cadet's family and their propensity for practical jokes. The whole row had obviously been got up on purpose, he said, with a view to the production of the eighteenth-century manual and its instruction on blowing off in the ranks – which was good for a brisk laugh, and God how they all needed one. Clearly a man of taste, Peter averred; it would have been amusing to know his view of Bowra's essay in pastiche, had the thing only gone that far.

'All right,' I said: 'a soldier. You just said that Bowra was also a poet?'

'That,' said Peter, giggling ferociously, 'is another story.'

'Tell. Please.'

'All right. If you will go back to Saunderites [my House], brush your hair, wash your face, tie your tie properly, and polish your shoes, I'll tell.'

So half an hour later Peter began:

'It all started with Beresford's *Sonnets of Shakespeare*, a work of which you will not yet have heard . . .'

T. Stewart Beresford, it seemed, had been a don in one of the very minor Oxford Colleges. Elected to a Life Fellowship in 1854, he had spent the next forty years translating Shakespeare's Sonnets into Latin Elegiac Verse, an achievement that much recommended him to Peter. The results were published in a private and limited edition printed on vellum, at the rate of one sonnet to the page on the left, one Latin Version to the page on the right.

'But the trouble was,' said Peter, 'that it just wasn't good enough for the sole work of forty years . . . though I suppose that in those days most dons who had security of tenure did nothing at all. At least T. Stewart Beresford had done something. But he hadn't done it very well. One version – that of the Sonnet which begins "No longer think of me when I am dead" – was truly excellent. Two or three were at least passable. But none of them was a patch on Housman's dedicatory Latin Verses at the beginning of his edition of Manilius, and some of them were positively risible.'

On the other hand, there was no denying that, in the printing and in general presentation, the Beresford edition was a handsome, nay a sumptuous volume . . . his grandfather's copy of which was given to Peter, at his special request, on his twenty-first birthday. Many years later, when Bowra was visiting Charterhouse as the Headmaster's guest early in the war, he came to take tea with Peter, spotted the Beresford edition, which he had heard of but never seen, and asked if he might take it back to the Headmaster's House for the two remaining days of his visit. Permission granted – and not, as so often in such cases, abused. The book was returned by Bowra in person an hour or two before his departure, whereupon Peter put it back on his shelves and thought no more about it for that time.

[70]

'Can I look at it?' I said now.

'I'm afraid not. You'll understand why when I've finished the story.'

The next occasion for fetching out Beresford's *Sonnets of Shakespeare* had been only a few weeks later, in response to a request from the Uncle, who had set the Classical VIth 'When forty winters shall besiege thy brow' to turn into Latin Elegiacs and was eager to examine Beresford's version.

'Here you are,' said trusting Peter to the Uncle. '"When forty winters" is one of his better efforts.'

'What a shplendid book,' the Uncle had said.

He often pronounced 's' as 'sh'.

'Yes, yes, isn't it? The last person to borrow it,' said Peter with stars of hero-worship in his eyes, 'was Maurice Bowra.'

'I am proud to be his successor,' said the Uncle, who did not hold Bowra in the same esteem as Peter did.

That evening the Uncle was back.

'Did you know,' he said, 'that Bowra wrote poetry?'

'I think I did. Alan Pryce-Jones once told a friend of mine that Maurice kept what Alan called a "bottom drawer" full of verse. Alan said he'd actually seen inside it on some occasion or other, but had had no time to read any of the stuff. All that he could be certain of was that there were a lot of loose pages with stanzas written on them.'

'Pages like thish one?' said the Uncle grimly.

He passed over a sheet of paper to Peter. On it were the following lines, signed M.B.

> *Lines Written at Charterhouse*
> In summer time on Maniacs*
>   Is sound of bat and ball;
> The flannelled boys are playing there,
>   Willowy and tall;

* Maniacs, a cricket ground at Charterhouse (now as then) used by an eponymous team which approximates to a 4th XI.

And one goes in to stop the rot,
  The last Forlorn Hope,
A fair and bold and bonny boy,
  Who does not scratch and grope

(As many would in such a case)
  But leaps the ball to smite
And cracks it o'er the boundary
  With speed of summer light,

And cracks again, and smashes far:
  The fieldsmen, full of dread,
Do step by step themselves withdraw
  To limit of the mead,

Until a mighty cheer goes up
  From those around the pav:
The runs have mounted six by six
  Till passed the foes' they have.

Thus has the one lad victory
  Snatched from the jaws of shame:
Ride forth, Saint George of England,
  And do the very same;

For Albion, now embattled sore,
  Needs shining knights and true,
Needs fair and bold and bonny boys,
  Brave cricketer, like you.*

'So we surmise,' said Peter to the Uncle, 'that Maurice Bowra, inspired by the sight of our boys at play, has written this – er – hymn to youth and courage, and left it in Beresford? I must admit to being rather disillusioned in the matter of Maurice's prosody, Uncle, to say nothing of his taste. But there is surely no need to look *quite* so censorious?'

* This poem has been transcribed from memory. It is possible that I have done the poet less than justice.

'Thish,' said the Uncle, 'ish only a rough draught. A final fair copy, with a message of gratitude to yourself for lending Beresford to him, and to the Masters and boys for their hospitality, has been inscribed on the title page. I always thought that Maurish Bowra thought rather too much of himself.'

'With full signature,' said loyal and quick-witted Peter; 'not just initials?'

'With full signature.'

'Then my book will double in value,' said Peter, determined to find what defence he could for Bowra. 'Maurice, after all, is a distinguished academic and literary figure. He has turned this volume into a *curiosity*. I *thought* he looked rather disappointed when I just took the book from him and put it straight away. I expect he hoped that I'd open it and see his – er – lucubration. Have you brought Beresford with you, by the way?'

'No,' said the Uncle. 'What I have told you so far is only by way of introduction. Beside this sheet there were several more, which must have been left there by accident. I had no time for more than a mere glance at them, as I was called urgently to Brooke Hall*, but I did establish that *theeshe* were parodies – and unlike Bowra's original verse they were of very high quality.'

'Better and better,' said Peter: 'rotten poets always make first-rate parodists. Remember Calverley?'

'Of very high quality,' repeated the Uncle, 'and of grave disrepute. One of T. S. Eliot, for example. You recall that passage in *The Waste Land* which has the refrain, "Here is only rock and no water", something of the kind? Well, Bowra conjures a distinguished colleague at Oxford, unnamed but undoubtedly, as one can deduce from a personal peculiarity, Rooksby, and then envisages him in a bistro in Paris trying to – er – pick somebody up. "Here is only cash but no credit," runs the parodied refrain. And of course Rooksby, who is famous for his parsimony, has not got any cash. Finally one of his companions consents to give him some Francs, in exchange for Rooksby's cheque drawn on his English bank and

* The Masters' Common Room at Charterhouse.

at an exorbitant discount. That sounds like Raymond Mortimer's kind of behaviour – and he is just the man to have been in this squalid gallery. Rooksby tries to wriggle out of actually writing the cheque until later, on the ground that his cheque book is back in their hotel, but the Mortimer figure knows his Rooksby and is adamant. So Rooksby, in the last stages of frustration, is sent scuttling back to the hotel. "Here is no credit, only cash." Eventually, just as the sun is rising outside the bistro, Rooksby charges through the door in a muck sweat, hands over the cheque and gets his Francs. Then the parody switches to another poem of Eliot's:

> ' "He grows old, he grows old,
> He likes the bottom of his prepuce rolled;
> But to no purpose, for he cannot rise
> Unless he is most violently chastised.
> So see him walk across the floor
> And cautiously select the toughest whore." '

'I see, Uncle. And what else did you find time to glance at in your haste?'

'A parody of Betjeman, I think it must be:

> ' "I think that I should rather like
> To be the saddle of a bike." '

'Oh. I thought that Betjeman actually wrote that himself, quite seriously.'

'And one of Tennyson's *In Memoriam*. Prudish little Attlee longs to get out of the Chamber in the House of Commons to go somewhere, and at last gets his chance at the end of Question Time,

> ' "And thought that here was luck indeed;
> But through the lavatory door
> Comes Winston, wet in mouth and maw
> With cognac, retching as he peed,"

[74]

and puts poor Clem off.'

'I can still discern nothing for you to look so severe about, Uncle, unless he's written these parodies all over the vellum pages . . . and even then the book would only become yet more of a curiosity, a real rarity. Manuscript examples of Bowra the would-be poet and Bowra the salacious parodist . . .'

'. . . As I told you,' said the Uncle, 'I was suddenly called to Brooke Hall. While I was away, my wife Mildred, who like all women after Eve hankers to put her nose where it isn't wanted, came into my study, examined Beresford, noted the tone and content of the parodies, and in a fit of righteousness flung the whole lot into the incinerator.'

'You mean,' said Peter faintly, 'that she flung the loose parodies into the incinerator?'

'No. Book and all. Perhaps she associated the parodies with the book itself, and was determined to punish that too; or perhaps she thought that some of them might actually be written in it, like the poem on the title page. God knows what manner of female imbecility came over her, my dear fellow, but she has destroyed everything. I shall of course be at full charges for your loss.'

'But that book,' Peter said to me now, 'was priceless and irreplaceable. So, come to that, were Bowra's parodies.'

Peter sniffed four or five times, in the famous and much imitated ('Sniffy') fashion.

'So there, dear boy,' he said, 'you have Bowra in his three characters of scholar, soldier and poet. And in a fourth – that of lampooner or satirist.'

'And in a fifth,' I said: 'that of satyr.'

'Satyr?'

'That poem about all those fair, flannelled and willowy boys.'

'Will you never learn,' said Peter, 'not to take things too far? *Convention* is very important, and *convention* decrees, quite rightly, the scruffy hobbledehoys should not impute criminal vice to their seniors. *I* am inhibited from so speaking by charity and taste. *You* are quite simply forbidden such speech. In each case convention has laid down the law. Now then, Simon: you will be forgiven just about everything in this world if only you will obey convention; you will be crushed if you flout it. A man will forgive your manifest adultery with his wife, and even your seduction of his virgin daughters, far sooner than he will forgive your wearing a dinner jacket when his invitation has specified tails.'

In this manner did V. S. (Peter or 'Sniffy') Russell, by a combination of instruction, entertainment and love (for love there was on my part at least) bring me back from the valley of the shadow.

MANY YEARS LATER, Robert Birley told me of the manner of Peter Russell's death, which occurred in the late fifties. Before Robert told me the tale, all I knew was that Peter had died of heart failure; but the actual circumstances, as described by Robert, combined comedy, irony and pathos in so nice a ratio that I should like to recall them here.

Robert Birley had been present, one summer's afternoon, at a performance of the Charterhouse Masque, a pageant which used to take place at the school annually (does it still?) for the celebration of Old Carthusians, their virtues and knaveries.

'Peter had always longed to play Judge Jeffreys,' Robert told me, 'and to my delight, there he was doing it. But as his face worked more and more fiercely in mock commination, I said to myself, "Steady on, old chap, you're starting to overdo it. You're 'enjoying yourself too much', as they say in the theatre." But of course he wasn't enjoying himself at all: he was in the spasms of a cardiac crisis and was dead before they got him into the wings.' Robert smiled. 'One minute he was being so funny,' he said, 'and the next he was dead. What a splendid way to go before his God.'

I have never forgotten this comment by one truly Christian man upon another.

R ATHER MORE than a year after being rescued from the pit by Peter Russell, I was once again on the verge of triumph. In my third cricket season I had had an all-round success which culminated in a trial for the first XI. A practice run, in December, for a Scholarship at Corpus Christi, Oxford, while not fetching an award, had gone quite creditably. In March of 1945 I was told I should be made a House Monitor (first step towards real power and place) at the beginning of the Cricket Quarter; and in April I had won a Foundation Scholarship at King's College, Cambridge (far more my sort of galley than Corpus in the other place). I was warming up very nicely; the dreary months through which Peter Russell had nursed and succoured me were receding fast.

I now saw rather less of Peter, who kept warning me against the infatuation and conceit which had undone me two years before, and a great deal more of my contemporaries, who once again found me acceptable. Thus I was poised on the brink, not yet carried over it (as I soon would be) by the further success that was to follow but still nicely balanced and treading warily, still just mindful enough of the bad times to eschew any act that might invite their return, still quick to stop my ears against the serpent . . . who several times, during this period, tried hard to coerce me. Two such occasions were while I was up at King's taking the scholarship examination, the first of these at the coffee party which the Provost gave for all candidates.

'When I was a boy,' said the Provost *ex cathedra*, 'they ground me at grammar but did not quite break me. That is how our middle class public schools proceed. Mine [Dulwich] was one of the lesser middle class schools, and so all the more insistent on painful tasks and conventions. Although I have remained very attached to it (for some days were happy there) I have never forgiven it for the grinding I got. It was as though they were saying, "Just because you are reading ancient literature and not some grimy subject like chemistry, just because you are preparing for Cambridge and not for an apprenticeship in accountancy or a stool in a bank, *you need not think that your studies are to yield you pleasure*. They could do – we know that. But we are determined that they should not. Nor

[77]

do we want any signs from you of temperament, originality (another word for irregularity), emotion, or enthusiasm for strange byways. We shall keep you to the routine 'Hammer, Hammer, Hammer on the hard high road': no 'hunting in the hills' for you." '

The Provost's fine white mane of hair gleamed like the beacon that announced victory at Troy to Clytemnestra; his trouser leg had ridden up to reveal a prosaic passage of long grey pant above his grey wool socks. Such a beautiful face, I thought, such dowdy ankles. The Provost proceeded:

'But, as I have said, I was not broken. I eluded the grind, I covertly exchanged the "hard high road" for the soft, green hills. For Mount Ida. And there I saw Paris with the Apple. As you will remember, there were three goddesses in contention for this: Hera, the Queen of Olympus; Athena, the goddess of wisdom (and of shift); and Aphrodite, laughing Aphrodite, the goddess of love. It was to her that Paris gave the Golden Apple: heedless of the Place that Royal Power might have bestowed on him, spurning the privilege that he might have had through cultivating craft and wisdom, Paris chose Love.

'I saw him and applauded. So, when I came to this college, I too had chosen Love. And here I found it. An old story, which I need not retell:

'"Young Apollo, golden haired,
    Free from trouble and from strife,
Magnificently unprepared
    For the long littleness of life."

But life was neither little nor long for *my* Apollo. He sang beautiful songs in his youth and was early claimed by death, when fighting for his King. His memory abides. But, had I not broken free from my mentors on that hard high road, I should never have known my Apollo, or only from afar. There would have been no ecstasies and no memories – had I not cast away the Glommery and followed the Muses.'

[78]

So what he is saying, I thought to myself as I came away and walked on the gravel path between the lawn and the Cam, what he is saying is that we are to throw the book of grammar (glommery) and seek out poetry . . . and through poetry Love. Love? Laughter and Desire in the shady places of the Garden, or abiding adoration in the Temple? He was not specific. 'Memories and ecstasies' could comprehend either. Nor need either necessarily preclude the other.

But in any event whatever, I thought to myself by the river, his advice is dangerous. He recommends one to skimp one's work and hang around to see what amusements are going and whom one can pick up (so much for the 'soft, green hills' and for 'Paris on Ida'). It is just *that* sort of behaviour (among other things) that got me into trouble last time; thinking myself so clever that I could get away with anything.

I was joined by a friend that I had made on the trial run at Oxford. He too had predictably failed there among the Puritans and was now trying to join the Athenians at King's. He came from Bradfield, was called Anthony Fijis. Someone else whom I knew from Bradfield had told me during the holidays that there was something suspect about Fijis, something odd that had happened before he came to Bradfield at the *advanced age of fifteen*, nobody knew what. Deciding that this would be as good a time as any to find out, if I could only twist the discussion in that direction, I began to listen carefully, with this in mind, to the second serpent of the evening.

'That old man was of course referring,' said Anthony Fijis, 'to Rupert Brooke. Rupert of Rugby and King's, the most celebrated beauty of his day. But I'll tell you some things about Rupert. My mother,' said Fijis with a dogmatic air, 'used to move in select circles in London where literary – and other – matters were shrewdly discussed. And the first thing she found out about Brooke was that his poetry would never have lasted had he not died in the war. The later stuff would have gone off, if he'd lived, and thus discredited the earlier, which is in any case pretty discreditable and has been allowed to survive only out

[79]

of respect for a dead hero. Or, more accurately,' said Fijis, cleaving the air fiercely with his scimitar nose, 'out of respect for a man whom the intelligentsia had decided to set up for a hero, as a matter of policy, during a period when it was seriously hard up for heroes in its own ranks. If only it could show a few *bona fide* heroes, you see, among poets and painters and so forth, in a really exciting and romantic aura, then the bulk of the Bloomsbury lot could just go on funking and skiving well out of the limelight while everyone else watched (so to speak) their 1st XI in action . . . a side for which they sorely needed Rupert Brooke. But once they had had him set up as a hero, then even after he was dead – especially after he was dead – they had to go on paying lip-service to his poetry, which all of them really hated for reasons ranging from pure envy to genuine critical distaste.'

'What charming friends your mother must have,' I said.

'Actually, yes. Eddie Marsh, etiolated Eddie, was one. *He* thought Brooke was a very fine poet, but he still used to tell my mother the nasty things which most people were saying about him in secret. And another of the things they were saying,' said Fijis, his nose curving down (almost into his throat, it seemed) from the middle of his poker face, 'was that although Rupert had a very beautiful face, he had simply *appalling* legs. Fibrous and chunky, going in and out at all the wrong places.'

'Do you suppose . . . that he did it . . . with the Provost?'

Careful, careful, I told myself, the poison in the tongue is beginning to work; though I am as yet innocent of infatuation or conceit, this is *not* the sort of conversation that a Monitor elect should be having.

'It seems that no one was ever quite sure. It's pretty certain that Brooke, at least, did it with several other people. You knew I was at Dartmouth before going to Bradfield?'

Ah, I thought, here comes the secret, the something suspect I had been warned of in the holidays. A great piece of luck, which I had so far done nothing to deserve. Careful now. Softly, softly catchee Fijis.

'I knew you arrived at Bradfield when you were already fifteen,' I said.

'I started by going to Dartmouth at twelve and a half. Then it suddenly occurred to my mother, really rather late in the day, that as a Cadet at the Royal Naval College I should get into the war much younger than anybody else. I should pass out of the place as a midshipman at seventeen or so and be mid-shipped straight into a battleship – or so she thought.'

'What's all this got to do with people doing it or not doing it with Rupert Brooke?' I said.

By now it was already clear that Fiji's secret was going to be pretty commonplace; the topic of Rupert Brooke's sexual career, on the other hand, inflammatory and therefore forbidden as it was, was irresistible.

'Patience, dear boy. My mother decided that I must leave Dartmouth, and took me away at once. Since we were at war, this was regarded by the authorities as an act of cowardice and desertion. They refused to co-operate in getting me in to anywhere else.

'But at about this time Eddie Marsh introduced my mother to one of the classical masters at Bradfield. This fellow, X, was forty odd and longed to go to war with the Navy, but of course they wouldn't have him. Reserved occupation, they said, and what could we do in the Navy with a middle-aged officer who knew nothing but Latin and Greek? Why was he so anxious to go, my mother asked him, and why the Navy?

'And then it turned out that he had been at Cambridge with Rupert Brooke (though a good deal younger and in a different College) and he wanted to be in the Navy because, while he himself had been just too young for the first war, Rupert, who had died in it, had endured most of his fatal illness on board a warship. No, it wasn't, said my mother: it was a troop transport, or else a hospital ship. Which came to the same thing, said this dominie, and what did it matter in any case as he wouldn't be going in one? My mother then asked him a lot of questions about what Rupert had been like when they were at Cambridge, and at last elicited (she is a *very* persistent woman) that the dominie, one shameless

[81]

summer evening long ago, had embraced a willing though fully dressed Rupert in the bottom of a punt.

'My mother then asked him a lot more questions, in an effort to establish where this had happened (near Grantchester perhaps), what clothes, if any, had been removed, and whether or not either of them had come, and if so how. After a lot of trouble and a good deal of Eddie Marsh's gin, she succeeded in getting the man into gear. But just as he was about to spill the jism (so to speak) Eddie Marsh came in. He'd been out of the room most of the time while my mother had been grilling the dominie, but now he gavotted through the door and said to Mama . . .

' "I think I've fixed it. X's being here made me think of it. Would Bradfield do for Anthony?"

' "Anything would do for Anthony," my mother said. "I'm desperate. He's drooping around at home like a drowning Ophelia."

' "Right," said Eddie. "Chap I know on Winston's Staff knows the Headmaster, and he'll manage it, whatever they say at Dartmouth."

'So mother had had an immense piece of luck,' said Fijis to me, 'getting me off her hands against all the odds, but she never found out the prime dirt about Rupert Brooke and X the dominie, because as soon as X realised that she had a son who was about to go to Bradfield, he absolutely shut up like a dead mussel. So alas,' said Fijis, 'we shall probably never know. They do say that the University Librarian, who is a Fellow of this College, has a pair of Rupert's underpants, which he stole as Rupert was bathing naked in the river, but he sounds a pretty shabby sort of chap, thieving like that, and not the kind to have reached the right true end of love with Rupert.'

'But the sort of chap that might have been watching from behind the azaleas when Rupert reached it with others?'

'Can you imagine working round to the subject with a sixty-year-old librarian?'

'If he really has a pair of Rupert Brooke's underpants he must be predisposed towards such discussions.'

[82]

'All right,' said Anthony Fijis: 'you take it on. You could pretend to be friendly – *extra* friendly – and then . . .'

'*Retro Satanas*,' I said, and went off to bed before the honey-voiced serpent could talk me into talking myself out of a Scholarship at King's and my seat at the Mos' (Monitors') table.

THUS I LISTENED to two serpents at Kings, both of whom spoke dangerously of worldly and pleasurable ways and, even more dangerously, of the delights of knowing best for oneself, of plausibly reasoned disobedience (throw away the dead grammar books they give you and seek the living Muse). But this, I knew, was that deadly 'first disobedience', which led to the eating of

> '. . . the fruit
> Of that forbidden tree, whose mortal taste
> Brought death into the world and all that woe.'

The serpents' message, then, I (temporarily) rejected. But I did hear and heed, during that visit to King's, another message, that of a just man, D. W. (Donald) Lucas, who interviewed me during the course of my exam.

Donald was a very dry scholar, but he was blessed with the empirical leanings of the true Rugbeian and a persistent hankering to qualify and soften the stark commands of Thomas Arnold with the beguiling discourse of Matthew – another Rugbeian tendency noted earlier in these pages. When I went to see him, I was asked of the extent of my official reading in the classics (under Peter and the Uncle) and of my own private reading, both in the classics and elsewhere. Elsewhere I was strong on nineteenth-century poets and novelists (the Uncle's influence) and in the classics I could

[83]

boast private reading of Propertius, Homer, Apuleius and Tacitus.

'No Greek drama?' enquired Donald, in a neutral voice.

'No,' I said; 'I don't much care for Greek plays. Or Latin ones, come to that.'

'One may ask why not?'

'The methods are so irritating and artificial. Those endless choruses of priggish disapproval. Or the Messenger Speeches; very fine, some of them, but leaving us frustrated – with a desire actually to see what we have only heard.'

'Unreasonable,' said Donald: 'they did not have cinema screens.'

'Granted, sir.'

'But your point about the choruses is interesting,' Donald said. 'While crude and frivolously founded, it does make a legitimate criticism of Greek Tragedy: the choruses, at any rate of the earlier Tragedies, will insist on laying down the moral law, whereas these days an audience prefers to apply its own moral law, though sometimes consenting to revise it. But what no one, nowadays, will stand for, is being told what to think, as one is told by so many Greek Choruses.'

'And yet,' said Donald, 'are modern audiences altogether wise in this? When I first came to this College I had a friend that had come here from a school called St Lawrence, on the south-east coast of Kent. It was a Fundamentalist school. Masters had been sacked for even hinting that the account of the Creation in Genesis need not be taken *au pied de la lettre*. Immoderate in this respect, it was definitely moderate in every other. Most of the boys were local and left at seventeen to work in offices or in their parents' orchards. Very few came to Cambridge and almost none to King's. My friend was entirely untypical, having been sent to St Lawrence only by mistake. His father, a builder of bridges and dams in India, had confused it with Lancing, also on the coast. Not,' said Donald, 'that my friend would have been much better off at Lancing; but at least the story explains the almost unique phenomenon of a Laurentian's arriving at King's, which to St

[84]

Lawrence is a kind of Rome-cum-Babylon-cum-Cities-of-the-Plain.

'Unlikely as it might seem, he told me, there were pleasures to be had at St Lawrence, or at least compensations for the strictness and dreariness of the place. Not the least of these was *mental ease*. There were no decisions to be taken at St Lawrence; whatever your predicament, you simply consulted the Bible, a form of the old Sortes Biblicanae, though passages were selected by rote rather than at random. Should one study history or science? Look in the book of Ecclesiastes, which was informative as to choice of careers. Should one go out or stay in? See the book of Proverbs, which was full of admirable advice about domestic and everyday behaviour. The whole point was that it was never necessary to *think*. No agonising about anything. The Bible, if correctly consulted, would tell one, on every conceivable occasion, what to do, where to go, what to feel, how to judge.

'Now perhaps it was rather the same,' said Donald, 'for ancient Greeks who *accepted* the authority of the Tragic Chorus. They knew exactly where they were. The early choruses of Aeschylus, for example, announced a set of solid and obligatory moral attitudes towards all the events of the plays: you are to remember that the gods always resent and usually punish pride or exaltation in success; that it is wrong to murder your husband, however viciously he may have injured you; that it is wrong to murder your mother even if she has murdered your father, though this offence, like most, may be palliated if committed by command of a god; that justice must be informed, not by compassion but by reasoned equity; and so on. Accepting these judgments, everyone felt safe. They had the authority of myth; they told – they commanded – you what to think at any juncture, with a fair warning that if you presumed to use your own head in such matters, you might well get it cut off.

'Later dramatists, however, did not offer such certainty. Take *The Philoctetes* of Sophocles. This is a play about the claims of friendship versus those of official duty. The Chorus is one of sailors who are employed only to carry messages; neither they nor anyone else is working, or even pretending to work, within a defined frame of moral reference; no hard and fast rule of conduct is laid down by anybody; no one is either to praise or to blame for anything that occurs. In the end the muddle becomes so intolerable that a god from a Machine has to descend to clear it up.

'Now, conceding that the second type of play, which allows and indeed invites the judgment of the audience, is preferable to modern tastes, we must still ask ourselves whether there is not *something* to be said for the first, which leaves the spectators in no doubt as to the morality that regulated the dramatist's creation and so, by extension, ought to regulate his conduct – and their own.

'My friend from St Lawrence used to make roughly the same comparison between the iron biblical law of his school, which dictated every thought and action, and the liberal and tolerant standards of this College, which left all decisions of any kind strictly to the individual concerned. That the former case may often be the more comfortable, to say nothing of the more profitable, is demonstrated by a simple tale:

'My friend – let us call him Sanders –' (Donald Lucas said) 'was much given to fishing – coarse, fresh-water fishing. He particularly enjoyed spinning for pike. The idea of deceiving the fish into taking a piece of whirling metal which concealed a hook for an object of edible prey, this tickled his fancy. The process required skill, the exercise was beneficial, and the fresh air was salubrious. Since he was no good at ball games or athletics, this pastime was essential to his health.

'No fault was found with it at St Lawrence. The Bible was quite clear in such matters. To hunt and kill a living creature that might be eaten (as might most fish from rivers and lakes, and certainly the pike) was taken as common practice. To hunt for pleasure was at least condoned. Safe in the approval of Holy Writ, Sanders spent five happy years fishing at St Lawrence, and keenly looked forward to tackling new water in the fens round Cambridge.

'But, when he came to King's, his age of innocence was over. The first thing he learned here was that all one's actions must be scrutinised by conscience in the light of humanist morality, of

[86]

humane feeling and concern. This rule beyond doubt precludes deliberate acts of cruelty towards animals and abominates any pleasure which a human being might take in such acts; but, unlike the old biblical law, it then leaves a large area for intellectual and moral debate; it promotes doubt and insinuates qualification.

'The Bible says either "You can" or "You can't". In the case of hunting and fishing it said "You can". Now, if only the new code had said equally clearly "You can't", then Sanders would probably, if reluctantly, have accepted this. But the new code said nothing of the kind. It said that you couldn't be cruel for sport, but that a wise human custom allowed men to kill animals to eat. It also went on to conjecture whether a fish, being cold-blooded and having a very crude nervous system, could actually feel pain; and it remarked that a certain number of fish *must* be killed in certain rivers to avoid over-crowding and disease. In short, humanist instruction in the matter was exceedingly vague and (perhaps deliberately) gave no assistance.

'In the end, Sanders settled with himself that he could go on spinning for pike providing he knew that they were going to be eaten. As you may know, pike are not easily edible unless comprehensively filleted or turned into a kind of soufflé called a "quenelle". The skill required for either operation is highly specialised: Sanders did not possess it. The College Chef might, but it would take up too much of his time. Pre-war restaurants in the town did not go in for this kind of rarity. Meanwhile, the pile of pike in the College refrigerator (where Sanders was kindly allowed to deposit his catch) grew, grew stale, grew noxious. The pike had to be thrown out, not one of them eaten. Sanders comforted himself by the thought that he had at least *intended* them to be eaten. If only he could go on putting them in the College refrigerator, the pretence could be maintained and his sport could continue. But no. The Steward, having got rid of the first heap, would harbour no more of Sanders' dead pike.

'Perhaps, then, he could get the local river board to declare that they needed the fish population to be reduced? Alas, the board was too ill-informed to know whether it did or did not.

[87]

'Then perhaps biologists could assure him that pike did not feel pain when hooked? One said one thing, one said another. There was no *certainty* anywhere.

'Finally, Sanders tortured himself into a nervous breakdown, and was told by a kindly and sensible psychologist that if he did not go fishing he would not recover, and that his sanity must take precedence, in the moral scale, over the rights (whatever these might be) of fresh-water fish. Then the thing was at last solved, but only after Sanders had passed through many weeks of agony. So you see . . . perhaps better a dogmatic moral or religious ruling from the start than an appeal to human reason or conscience. Perhaps better nagging choruses than no guidance; perhaps, in the end, better St Lawrence than King's.'

'You can't believe that, sir,' I said.

'No. But there *is* a moral in the story.'

'Tell me, sir, why was your friend Sanders so quick to accept the prevailing system? I mean, at St Lawrence he accepted without question that the Bible had all the answers: but the moment he came here he subjected himself to the demands of liberal theory and personal conscience. Why so docile?'

'He was the kind of person that likes to please. So he always adopted the local practice, whatever it happened to be.'

'But to have a nervous breakdown . . . because he couldn't be certain what local or liberal practice might require in his treatment of fish . . . surely overdoing it?'

'He was, quite simply, a thoroughly decent man. And like many decent men he was a great fool. At bottom, he really wanted to be *told*. And so he was,' said Donald; 'he ended up in a strict order of monks among whom, except on certain Saints' days, the Abbot was the only person allowed to speak. However, fishing in the local streams and pools for the community kitchen was permitted and even exiged.'

A ND THEN I went home, and in due course was told that I
was now a Scholar Elect of King's. In May I won a rich and
prestigious Essay Prize; in June I received my cricket colours for a
tidy all-round performance in the Eton Match; a little later I was
told to prepare myself to be Head Monitor of my House at the
beginning of the next quarter but one; in July I made 50 odd
against the MCC and thought I should be chosen for the Southern
Schools against the Northern at Lord's.

I now became so full of myself and my achievements that I
abandoned all social decorum, moral restraint, attention to my
school work (what need had a Scholar of King's to work?) and even
residual discretion . . . with the result that I came humiliatingly
low in the Annual Examination of the Classical VIth, was again
much hated in all quarters, for that and other reasons (I wasn't
really any good) did *not* play for the Southern Schools at Lord's,
made myself intolerable to my family with my airs and pretensions
all through the summer holiday, and was expelled in tears and
squalor, just as the leaves began to fall, in the Oration Quarter.

And bloody well serve me right.

A ND SO, in the bitter January of 1946, instead of sitting
snugly in my study in Saunderites as Head Monitor, bidding
one go and he goeth and another come and he cometh, I was living
in a Nissen hut on Barnby Moor by Retford, with thirty other
National Service recruits. Of these, twenty-five were working
class boys who had been conscripted, while the other five were
approximately of the middle class and had 'volunteered', which
simply meant that we had signed up earlier than we were strictly
required to and had thus acquired the right of choosing our
regiments.

I had chosen the Parachute Regiment. Thither I should be sent

[89]

at the end of my six weeks of Primary Training on Barnby Moor
. . . for the purpose of which we were in the charge of a mixed bag
of officers and NCOs, most of them Riflemen. This meant, even
after five years of war and a dismal depression in the standards of
the British Army as a whole, that they were fine soldiers, sympathetic and tolerant instructors, and that the officers were also
gentlemen.

Our Platoon Commander was an Old Etonian called Waldo
Farquarson-Sale, and on the morning after our arrival, before we
had even been given our uniforms, he addressed us as follows:

'None of us wants to be here in this perfectly horrible place, but
the alternative is a civil or military prison. So we must just make
the best of it. If we try hard, we shall keep out of trouble and may
conceivably enjoy ourselves; we shall at least make the time go
faster.

'My advice to all of us is to stay in our respective places, keep our
mouths shut, and do precisely what we are told to do, no more and
no less. This is known as keeping our noses clean: there is a lot to
be said for it.

'We all of us have two consolations. First, it is no longer
probable and it is scarcely even possible that we should be called
upon to die for our country. Secondly, however nasty post-war life
in our country may prove, however idiotic the politicians, however tiresome the Unions, however greedy and useless the proverbial
man in the street, we in the Army are the last people that will starve
or freeze, no matter what the disasters for others.

'And most of you have one more thing to be thankful for. You
have no responsibilities whatever except to turn yourselves out
properly. *I* do not have to turn myself out properly: I have a
servant to do it for me. This is because I have to spend all my time
worrying about people like you, and how to keep you safe and
happy, and so must not be distracted by tedious chores such as
shining my own shoes or pressing my trousers. You see the point?
Others serve me in order that I may serve them.

'This is a sensible contract, but one which most people, these
days, wish to repudiate. To serve, in the sense of being a personal

[90]

servant to somebody, is considered servile. All very stupid. When I was a boy at school, I was somebody's fag: I made his toast, blacked his boots, cleaned out his study, ran his messages. In return he gave me small sums of money, protected me from the beastliness of the world outside, and effectively helped to run the school on which I depended for my education. I had a good contract: so have you. Keep your part of it, and you may hope to receive kindness and consideration: break it, and you may hope for nothing but misery.

'But, while most of you will have no responsibilities except to stay clean and obedient, some of you may be called to office of one kind or another. The following five recruits' – whereupon he named myself and the four other middle-class numbers – 'will now stay behind with me. The rest of you may dismiss to the NAAFI for mid-morning refreshments. If you please, Sergeant . . .'

'SIR.'

A cane-carrying Sergeant herded away the herd.

'So,' said Farquarson-Sale, beckoning the five others to come closer, 'the bourgeoisie is left behind in a cold, bleak lecture room, while the underdogs are released to receive cakes and ale. Lesson number one, gentlemen: privilege has its price. Not that any of you is yet privileged, but you may become so. All five of you are pricked on the roll as potential officers or NCOs. If you wish, you may elect to be officially regarded as candidates for Emergency Commissions, which means that in due course, if your superiors find no reason to revise your status, you will be sent before a series of boards which will either pass you on to an Officer Cadet Training Unit or send you back thither whence you came. In a moment I shall ask each of you whether he wishes to become such a candidate; but, before I do so, I must ask your attention to a cautionary tale.

'I was talking just now of my time as a fag at Eton. Pray notice that I name the school to you, whereas I did not do so before the rest of the Platoon: already the conspiracy of class has begun. Now, the fellow for whom I fagged, at the age of fourteen, was called Hereward Boyce, a lithe and sinewy lad of seventeen and a half, of some distinction as a Wet Bob, that is to say as an oarsman, but not of enough charm and/or importance to be elected to the Eton Society, that is to say Pop.

'Pop, as you may know, is a group of senior boys, self-elective and self-perpetuating, which in effect governs the entire school. This is a great trouble to a certain kind of Headmaster, who would wish to appoint the members of such a body himself. At all other schools the Headmaster appoints the School Prefects or Monitors: why not at Eton? Why, such a Headmaster would argue, should he depend, in matters of discipline, on boys who have been chosen at the whim of other boys? Many Headmasters have hankered to destroy Pop, or at least to have some say in the choosing of its members . . . only to find, as "whipping" John Keate found early in the nineteenth century, that while upper-class parents will allow middle-class ushers to flog their boys' buttocks, they will not tolerate officious or self-righteous interference with their own and their boys' *order*. An usher, you see, is simply a paid servant: he may and should correct in minor matters but he must always defer in great.

'So in the end each Headmaster reaches an unspoken agreement with the Eton Society, an agreement which has been compared to that between the church and the Baronage in the Middle Ages. Let Pop be responsible for day-to-day governance and the allotment of secular privilege, *provided* that its members pay lip-service, at least, to the moral doctrine propounded by the Headmaster and the Staff.

'But I digress, gentlemen. We were talking of my fag-master, Hereward Boyce, whom Pop had not co-opted. This was a grief to Boyce. In the first place, it called into question both his amiability and his adequacy. In the next place, it might seriously affect his chance in obtaining a commission in the Hussar Regiment of his choice. There was particularly hot competition for commissions in this regiment, much of it from Etonians. If the Colonel of the Regiment had had his way, he would have accepted all the Etonians before he even considered anyone else, but the Army Council, in its tiresome war-time affectation of democracy, had decreed that 50% of the appointments must go to boys from schools other than Eton and a minimum of 5% to boys from Grammar or Secondary Schools. This meant that only the cream of the many Eton candidates could be accommodated – and the cream meant Pop.

'There was to be an election for Pop about two months before Boyce must go to his interview with the Colonel. If he got into Pop, he would very probably be accepted for the regiment; if not, not. He didn't. Shame and Despair. He could, of course, try for the Guards, but the Household Cavalry, he reflected, were for good reason known as the Galloping Grocers, while the Foot Guards had certain nasty middle class habits such as calling their Commanding Officers "Sir" instead of "Colonel". No: it was the —th Hussars or nothing for Hereward Boyce . . . who then had a brain-wave.

'He would leave Eton and go to a Grammar School for a term. Candidates from Grammar Schools (*et cetera*) were entitled to 5% of the vacancies. The Colonel of the —th, he reasoned, would be so delighted to find someone that spoke the King's English to fill one of these vacancies that he would snap him up. A commission in the —th Hussars would amply compensate, in the scale of the world's esteem and his own, for his failure to become a member of Pop.

'And so it came about. How Boyce persuaded his parents, I do not know, but the next half found me without a fag-master and Boyce in a Midland Grammar School near his home in Rutland. The Colonel of the —th Hussars was delighted at the prospect of filling one place in his compulsory Grammar School quota with a fellow who was really an Old Etonian. As for the Etonian candidates, seven of them, including two that had been in Pop, they had to be rejected. Boyce had won hands down, so far.

'The only trouble was this. Although quite a decent chap and a very fair oarsman, Boyce had one appalling defect. This had nearly dissuaded me from becoming his fag, though in the end I decided that the privileges of the post outweighed my disinclination to its donor. It had certainly ditched him for Pop. For Boyce

[93]

was cursed with that particular kind of bad breath about which nothing whatever can be done. No amount of brushing and rinsing and gargling, no paste and no elixir, no process of purging the stomach or swabbing out the intestines, made the slightest difference. The debility could be neither explained nor cured. In one case only had it gone unnoticed: the Colonel of the —th, being a declining pantaloon who suffered badly from catarrh, had not so much as twitched a nostril.

'Boyce got through his early training in the Army without offending anyone, evil odours (as you will shortly discover) being the daily and therefore almost unnoticeable – certainly indistinguishable – concomitants of military life at that level. When he came to his War Office Selection Board he smelt, overwhelmingly and quite pardonably, of Jeyes or some similar fluid that must be frequently applied to some injury he had received.

'His breath was definitely noticed by the Cadets at his OCTU and also by his Platoon Commander, but it was felt by all that it would be unfair to complain of a man who tried so hard on such a relatively frivolous ground. And indeed Boyce's unfortunate peculiarity might have gone, not indeed without remark but without adverse consequence, for the rest of his Army career – had it not been for an Army Dentist who recommended a new concentrated mouthwash that might do the trick . . . and miraculously did, carrying a strong fragrance of Rose Essence which overcame, at last, poor Boyce's halitosis. It also caused his summary dismissal from OCTU by the Commandant, who, having sent for Boyce to congratulate him on his splendid record as a Cadet, noticed the smell of Boyce's new mouthwash and was convinced that he was wearing a woman's scent.

'Which is to warn you, gentlemen, of the cruel vicissitudes that your choice could bring upon you. Each rung in the ladder is more slippery than the last. Here are the necessary forms of application. Should you wish to go on with the thing, fill them up and return them within the week. Pray dismiss, gentlemen, except for Raven. I want a word or two with him.'

When the rest had shoved off, he said:

'What the devil's this? It *was* you playing for Charterhouse against Eton last summer? You caught Peter Blake, taking the catch on the wrong foot? You got two wickets because your breaks didn't work and the ball went straight through instead of coming in from the off? And you scratched a few runs like a demented hen before the match was rained off?'

'I got my colours for that match, sir,' I said.

'Then I wish you joy of them. But what on earth, dear boy, are you doing here? Somebody else watching that match – one of your people – told me that you had another summer at Charterhouse still to come. By which time you might be quite a decent player.'

'Things went wrong,' I said.

'I suppose you mean, "the usual thing" went wrong?'

'I suppose I do.'

'Well, *that's* what I've been working round to. Now. This business of a commission – I suppose you want one?'

'I suppose I do.'

'Well, the point is that at some stage you'll be required to get a Priest or a JP or something like that to sign a certificate saying that he's known you for some years and that as far as he knows you're morally respectable. The normal practice is to send it to one's old Headmaster for signature. But, if you've been in trouble at school for the usual thing, you can't do that, can you?'

'I suppose not.'

'So what shall you do?'

'I really haven't thought.'

'Then you'd better begin. There are several ways round this little difficulty, but I can't tell them to you, in case you get caught out and implicate me. However, I do not see why I should not tell you what happened, in this connection, to a chum of mine called Lumley Hall, and let you draw your own conclusions. Want to hear? Or would you sooner join your comrades in the NAAFI?'

'Anything but that.'

'I think you might call me "sir" rather more often. I know I'm only a year older than you, but I am an officer and you're not – not

[95]

by a very long chalk – and if I allow you to get away with slack discipline I shall be accused of class favouritism.'

'Who's going to accuse you . . . sir?'

'The others in the Platoon.'

'They can't hear us now.'

'Troops have the most devilish way of sniffing these things out. There's always one of them cleaning the windows or mending a door-knob or lurking up the chimney like a sweep, and if they see or hear anything irregular, like your not calling me "sir" often enough because we're both out of the same sort of bag, then off they go squealing about "privilege" all the way to their MPs. However, I don't think it can do any harm if I tell you about Lumley Hall. No ordinary soldier would understand the thing even if he overheard it. You have to have been at a public school to make any sense of it at all.

'Lumley was a chap who went to that school called R—. He was two or three years older than me, and lived near us in Norfolk. Wells-Juxta-Mare. Nice part of the world, lovely beaches and dunes and pine trees. Salt marshes. Bird sanctuaries. Just the sort of place that would have driven all those beastly city boys in the Platoon off their chumps. If they knew such a place existed, they'd probably complain to their MPs. Privilege again, you see: an insult, they'd call it, to anyone that lives in a town: one of these days they'll try to stop anyone at all, except registered farm labourers, from living in the country. Ever read Trollope? One of his characters, a millionaire who's got religion and social conscience very badly, says that we all ought to live in towns so that we should all know how wretched they are. But back to Lumley Hall.

'Lumley had a spot of the usual bother, like you did, and was pitched out of R— on his ear. At first he thought he might make use of this to pretend he was really queer and get out of National Service altogether. But his Governor was shrewd enough to spot what he was up to, and he told Lumley straight out that, if he tried that kind of a game, he'd be kicked clean out of the house and out of his pater's will.

' "I don't mind your playing with a few little boys' pricks,"

[96]

Lumley's pater said, "we've all been up to that at your age and bloody nice too; but I won't have you passing yourself off as a twenty-four carat Nancy Boy. You go off and do your bit in this war like everybody else. You come back with a commission like anybody else's boy, and I'll set you up all right afterwards – Oxford or whatever else you want. But just you start wagging your arse in front of the recruiting board and I'll put a pair of Purdies up it."

'So Lumley marched off with the Royal Marines, who took rather a shine to him, and said "Lumley, come up higher". It turned out that the Marines trained their own officers: they made you a probationary Second Lieutenant straight away, dragged you through every kind of shit and derision for a few months, and if you were still alive at the end of it they gave you a second pip and told you you were now pukkha. But, before you could go through all that, you had to get someone to sign this certificate about your morality, and here Lumley was in the same fix as you'll be in later on.

'He was given one of those certificates when he went on leave for the first time and told to get it signed before he came back. So he showed it to his Governor and suggested he might like to get one of his county chums to sign it – a High Sheriff or somebody like that.

' "Why not?" said Lumley's Governor, and drove off to Brancaster Golf Club (with his special Home Guard petrol ration) where he found the Lord Lieutenant. Better and better, he thinks: really send the boy off with a bang.

' "Would you sign this certificate for my boy, Lumley?" he says.

' "But your boy Lumley got the sack from R—," says the Lord Lieutenant.

' "He was only playing about," said Lumley's Governor, "like we all did at Harrow."

' "All right. But who shopped him?"

' "What does that matter?"

' "I mean, was he reported because he was a bully, or because he was a bore, or because he was careless, or because someone had a grudge? It does make a difference, you know."

[97]

' "According to his house-master's letter, the matron was inspecting the boys' rears, and heard a lot of panting behind one of the doors, and opened it, and found Lumley and some frightful brat red-handed."

' "So tasteless," says the Lord Lieutenant, "doing it in the rears. Couldn't they have found a bed, or a barn, or a shower, or something?"

' "No," said Lumley's pater. "Lumley explained all that. R— is one of those middle class schools where they have enormous sets of rules and regulations about buttons and ties and hats and where you can go if you're over sixteen and where you can't go if you're under fourteen and a half, and all that kind of thing."

' "Why did you send your boy to a middle class school? What was the matter with Harrow?"

' "Harrow's gone down hill, hadn't you heard? And the point about R— was that Hatty Driscol lives near there, and as you know I've always had a soft . . ."

' "All right. Get on with it. Where were we?"

' "Explaining why Lumley and his chum had to use the rears. That no one was allowed in anybody else's bed, of course, goes without saying. So when Lumley got the hots on he thought of the balcony in the squash courts, but Lumley's brat was too junior to be allowed up there. They thought of the place where the boats were kept, but since Lumley played cricket, he wasn't allowed on rowing premises. And so on and so forth. Either one of them was just too junior for this or the other was just too senior for that, and in the end they realised that the only place they were *both* allowed to be in was the House rears."

' "But surely not in the same compartment?"

' "Of course not. But at least they'd both be *in bounds* for boys of their ages."

' "But this is ridiculous," says the Lord Lieutenant. "You expect me to believe that your son, Lumley, and his – er – companion, who were about to break the most serious of all school rules, worried so much about trivial transgressions of trespass that they chose the nastiest possible place?"

' "Conditioning, I suppose. New boys at R— have to pass a prodigious examination about where they can go and where they can't, so I suppose that makes it stick. Anyway, it's just as well they *were* in bounds when they were caught, because if they hadn't been they'd have been flogged as well as sacked."

"So they were both sacked? The younger boy as well? I thought they usually let him off and only sacked his seducer."

' "The younger boy *was* the seducer. He made eyes at Lumley first."

' "But surely your son would have had the *chivalry* to take the blame?"

' "He would, but the younger boy was eager to claim full discredit. He wanted to be sacked, you see. He didn't care for R—."

' "I'm not surprised from what you say of it. But I'm afraid I just am not satisfied. Here's this brute of a son of yours, letting himself get used and seduced, behaving like an absolute *flop* during the entire business, and as good as sneaking on his poor little chum."

' "He didn't sneak. I told you, it was the poor little chum that claimed that *he* had hotted up *Lumley*."

' "Then Lumley should have denied it. He should have *played the man*. To sum the thing up, Hall: for an older boy to seduce a younger one is pretty well normal; but for a younger boy to seduce an older one is positively perverted of both of them, and Lumley should have put himself forward as the seducer if only to preserve face. Had he done so, I could have signed that certificate with a good conscience. As it is, no."

'After two or three more people had refused to sign for Lumley's character,' said Farquarson-Sale, 'time was running out. But the answer turned out to be surprisingly simple. One morning at the club Lumley's father saw someone put a sheet of paper in front of a retired judge and heard him say,

' "Sign there, please Hawkhurst. It's some piece of red tape rubbish for the Rural District Council. Need a chap of your standing to sign for my *bona fides*, ha, ha, ha."

[99]

'The judge signed without even looking and calmly accepted a very large drink.

'So the next day Lumley's pater wheeled up Lumley's certificate, and said,

' "Be a good chap and sign this, Hawkhurst. It's some piece of nonsense for the Army Council. Needs a senior man's autograph."

So again Hawkhurst signed without looking, probably thinking (if he thought at all) that this was something to do with the Home Guard, since Hall Senior was wearing the uniform of a Major in that outfit. Immediately on signature Hall bought Hawkhurst a large club measure (i.e. a double double) of pink gin. How much of the war effort that judge signed out of the window in return for pink gin' (said Farquarson-Sale) 'does not bear thinking about.'

'Well, what he signed for Lumley Hall's pater was really harmless enough, sir.'

'Except to Lumley Hall. He was killed off by a probationary Marine officers' exercise on Dartmoor. In those days, of course, simply a routine matter – they could kill pretty well whom they wanted in training, and no questions asked.'

'How did they kill Lumley Hall?'

'Exposure. Lumley read the map wrong one night and thought there was a shallow ford where there wasn't. By the time he found this out he was up to his waist in it. They wouldn't let him go back to base for dry kit ("This is WAR, boy"), so when they bivouacked he either had to sleep with his legs and bum bare under his single blanket or with his trousers freezing into ice on him. Disagreeable place, Dartmoor. You'll probably go on an exercise there if you get as far as OCTU.'

'What did Lumley do? About his trousers, I mean?'

'Kept them on. He had rather nice legs, you see, smooth and round, and he thought that if he showed them about while he was getting wrapped up in his blanket people would think he was trying to tempt them. And then he might lose his probationary commission. Probationary officers,' said Waldo Farquarson-Sale, 'could be broken overnight as easy as egg shells.'

'How do you know all this, sir?'

'He came home before he died, and I saw him once or twice. He'd had double pneumonia, been invalided out, and then come home to his father at Wells-Juxta-Mare. Before they could decide what his pension would be, he had to go before a medical board at the local depot in King's Lynn. They had him in naked, of course, and kept him hanging about in a draught while they thumped his chest and plumbed his navel, and the end of it was he caught pneumonia all over again and was dead in twenty-four hours.

'In all the circs there had to be an inquest – conducted by Judge Hawkhurst, who had been called out of his retirement to act as emergency war-time coroner. This meant, among other things, that Hawkhurst had to go through all Lumley's Army documents – which included the certificate of morality signed by Hawkhurst.

'Hawkhurst got into a royal bate with Lumley's father. He said he'd since heard the full story of Lumley's bad form from the Lord Lieutenant, and he certainly wouldn't have signed if he'd been honestly approached and realised at the time what he was signing. He even threatened to go to the Marines and have poor Lumley posthumously reduced to the ranks as having been commissioned under false pretences. But, when Lumley's pater said something nasty about double club measures of pink gin, he decided to drop that one.'

'Surely pointless in any case?'

'So you and I might think, but when these old swine get up on their moral high-horses, there's nothing they won't trample on. But Lumley, as I say, was let off and kept his rank in his coffin and was included in the Roll of Honour of the Royal Corps of Marines, 1939 to 1945.

'But, though he escaped the malice of Judge Hawkhurst, he got shat on from another quarter. When his Governor wrote to R— to put in the name of Second Lieutenant L. Hall, Royal Marines, for the School Memorial, he was informed that his son's name had been stricken from the record on the day when he'd been expelled, and that for the purposes of R— College he had then and there ceased to exist.

'So you see what may be in store for you,' said Farquarson-Sale kindly, 'if you persist in going after a commission.'

B UT PERSIST I DID, and in the December of 1946 found myself an Officer Cadet at the OTS in Bangalore, Mysore State, South India.

I have written a lot about what happened to me there; but now a tale or two of other people may serve to illustrate my present thesis, which is, very roughly, that public school boys daily commit, in the name of sanity, decency and loyalty, acts of such absurdity, perversity and spite that they are understandably regarded by much of the populace with horror and disgust.

I T WAS MY FORTUNE, when we arrived at Bangalore, to be allotted quarters in the same 'basha' as a cadet called Giles Freebody. One morning our Indian bearer produced for me two left-footed boots, one of which was Giles's, and for Giles two right-footed boots, one of which was mine. The matter was sorted out quite fast, but not before I had shouted very nastily at the poor little Indian (a memory which is still frequent with me and still makes me sweat with self-loathing). Giles very properly took me to task. He had been, as I knew, to a Roman Catholic public school (Ampleforth) and now treated me to a stiff helping of Papist precept.

'Your trouble is,' he said, 'that you regard that poor bloody Indian, and indeed everybody else, as just so much humanoid machinery to oblige, pleasure or obey you. He has a soul, as you do, and with that in common he is entitled to your civility and respect.'

After uttering several more sentiments of this order, he concluded by threatening to report me to our Company Commander if anything of the kind happened again.

'The Platoon Commander would perhaps be more appropriate,' he said, 'but he's only an Indian himself.'

'Report me?' I said. 'You mean *sneak* on me, Giles?'

'I do not understand the word "sneak".'

'It means to tell tales,' I said, 'to inform or delate, which is behaviour regarded with contempt by any gentleman who has been to a public school.'

'Not if he went to *my* public school,' said Giles. 'We were taught that it is our duty under God to report wrong doing and corruption.'

'You mean, some fucking priest got at you,' I said.

'If you like to put it so coarsely, yes.'

'But what sort of place was Ampleforth,' I said, 'if everyone was running round denouncing each other? It's the sort of thing that happens in Russia – and used to happen in Nazi Germany.'

'So at Charterhouse,' said Giles, 'you would not have reported cases of bullying or sexual exploitation?'

'We might have if it was very bad. Bullying, certainly. The other thing if somebody younger was *forced*. Not otherwise.'

'Then you were condoning mortal sin.'

'What sins people commit are their business.'

'No. They must be prevented from sinning lest they imperil their own souls and lead others to destruction.'

'What price the Inquisition?' I said. 'Did you have a torture chamber at Ampleforth? Or did all the dirt come out during confession?'

'What is disclosed to one's confessor,' said Giles, 'is inviolably secret.'

'But of course one could always be summoned by the priest *after* confession for a confidential talk. And since confidence may be abused by the priest if the confessional may not, should he think the moral reasons to be weighty enough,' I said, 'he can go straight off and blab to higher authority. Now, I suppose one can see that a *priest* might seriously consider this to be doing his duty. What I detest is the kind of *boy* who would blow the whistle . . . except, I grant you, in cases of physical or sexual cruelty, or theft, now I come to think of it. That's where I draw the line. Where do you draw it?'

'We don't. Even petty misdemeanour, we were taught, must be reported, in order that it may be punished for the good of the offender, and publicly unveiled for the warning and protection of others.'

'But you can't apply that rule to *everything*. You might, let's say, report somebody for cheating at work – but only if he was gaining marks and kudos at others' expense, *not* if he was just doing it to save himself from a whipping.'

'Any form of cheating is a form of lying,' said Giles: 'of course it must be reported.'

'Well then: cutting chapel. Would you report a fellow for that?'

'Yes – but we shouldn't need to. Surveillance in *that* area was particularly strict.'

'Cutting PT, then. Would you report a chap who got away with that?'

'Yes. It is his duty, especially in war time, to keep himself physically fit.'

'But Giles. If you're so certain that to report people is the right thing, why are you giving me another chance now?'

'Because despite your horrible behaviour this morning I quite like you,' said Giles.

'But surely, you're not meant to let anything as vain as human affection count in the scale?'

'No, but of course one does,' said Giles. 'And in any case I have one more reason.'

'Tell.'

'Very private.'

'I shan't blab.'

Nor have I until now, nearly forty years later, with Giles long dead.

'Then you should know,' said Giles, 'that in Catholic schools not only is what you call sneaking encouraged, but also spying and eavesdropping. And not just accidental spying or eavesdropping; one is encouraged, one is *commanded*, to insinuate one's eyes and ears into any place, no matter how private, where one suspects that there might be evil or even, as I told you just now, merely petty misdemeanour. Nothing is too small to interest the authorities: I remember one man was beaten for being too lavish in his application of loo paper . . .'

One day, Giles told me, his best friend, a contemporary called Greenacre, had taken him on one side while they were watching a cricket match near the end of Giles's second summer term, and told Giles that he had asked his father to take him away and send him to a non-Catholic school – Winchester, he hoped, or Eton.

'But they'll never allow that,' Giles had said.

'Whom do you mean by "they"?' Greenacre replied.

'The Church. The monks. The priests.' Giles gestured towards the school building. 'The whole establishment,' Giles said.

'Then "they",' said Greenacre, 'have nothing to do with it. My father and I will decide the matter between us. He, incidentally, is not a Catholic, but my mother is, so he was bullied into letting them make one of me. Not to make any bones about the matter,' Greenacre went on, 'I'm thinking of cutting the Roman Church altogether.'

'*Apostasizing*? But why?'

'Because I think that the whole thing is almost certainly rubbish. And it isn't decent – all this snooping and prying and peaching. *Not decent*. Now, it wouldn't matter if the Roman Church were simply ridiculous, as it is, so long as it didn't take the thing to excess and become *indecent* as well. The Church of England is perfectly all right in that way. Of course the doctrine is absolute nonsense, almost as insane as ours, but at least half of them know that, so they don't press the business too far. They let you take it or leave it. They mind their own affairs and expect you

[105]

to mind yours. They don't take themselves or their religion too heavily. In one word,' said Greenacre, 'they are moderate.'

'Why are you telling me all this?' Giles had said.

'Because I rather like you, and I want you to know that next September I shan't be here . . . with any luck. I should also like to ask you to do what I'm doing. You'd be doing us both a great favour,' Greenacre said to Giles, 'if you'd change to the same place as me.'

'And do you know,' said Giles to me now, as the evening shadows advanced along the veranda of our 'basha' and the silly bells tinkled through the jacaranda trees, 'I was tempted. Or rather, since I knew it was no good, that my parents would never allow it, I found it a delicious fantasy. Besides, if Greenacre liked me, I adored Greenacre. So, while I could not and would not commit myself, I tried to show him that I was sympathetic, a worthy confidant if not, in practice, an ally.

' "I think I understand," I said. "But what exactly brought all this on?"

' "It's been coming on for some time," Greenacre said. "There are some things my father has told me, some books he's given me to read . . . He is an intelligent and thoughtful man, you see, whereas my Catholic mother is just a stupid, quacking bitch.'

' "Why did he marry her?"

' "Because she was beautiful. And in those days she wasn't as priest-ridden as she is now."

' "What will *she* say if you do what you're planning?"

' "She'll raise the roof. Luckily my father has some money now. Until just the other day, all the money was hers, so that we had to do as she said. But now some aunt of my father's has left him quite a bit.'

' "Has she any idea at all what you're up to?'

' "No. And she mustn't have. Or not until it's too late for her to interfere. If she gets to hear of it too soon, she'll find some way of stopping it. You know what fiends women can be. So keep it very quiet. And please think seriously of doing the same."

' "But I'm afraid my parents wouldn't even consider it."

' "You'd be surprised," Greenacre said, "what you can do if you only try. But, if you don't want to, at least keep it secret."

'At first' (continued Giles Freebody on the darkened veranda, while the cicadas screeched and a monotonous chant rose from the bearers' compound) 'none of this seemed to involve me in any problems or trouble whatever. As for Greenacre's suggestion that I might go with him, though this was not without its attractions, I knew (or thought I knew) that in no circumstances was my father going to let me change schools and that there was no point in mentioning the matter to him (even had he been in England, which he wasn't), and that was all about that. As for keeping Greenacre's intentions secret, well, the official code had it that I should immediately rush to the nearest monk to denounce what he was up to; but this, I knew by instinct, would have been exactly what Greenacre himself had called "indecent", whatever the Church or the monks might say. Just you keep quiet, I told myself, and the whole thing will sort itself out without any skin off your nose. After all, who was I to start shouting the odds to anyone when Greencare was acting in consultation with his own father?

'But in all this I had reckoned without one thing. Unknown either to Greenacre or myself, our conversation had been partly overheard by a boy who was fielding not far from us on the boundary.'

Giles's dumpy face wobbled with retrospective apprehension.

'While he had not gathered the full enormity of Greenacre's plan,' said Giles, 'he had heard enough to realise that Greenacre, having somehow got hold of some subversive books, was seriously questioning Christian doctrine in general and Catholic doctrine in particular. He had not (it appeared) heard any of Greenacre's references to his father, because his duties in the field had much disrupted his attention to our duologue, but he had heard quite enough to know that Greenacre was deeply discontented with Ampleforth and its ethos, and was seeking some sort of escape. With this intelligence he hurried off, as soon as the match was done, to the Benedictine Father who acted as his spiritual director and also, as it happened, as mine and Greenacre's.'

Giles's brown curly hair crackled in the darkness with his disgust and indignation at the shabbiness of it all.

'A tormenting Inquisition now followed. Father Jeremy was a man of genial presence, worldly address, and rigid orthodoxy. Lulled into carelessness by the two former, one would suddenly be pinioned and mercilessly probed by the latter. What the good father wanted to know was (a) the full extent of Greenacre's subversive thought and intention, and (b) why I myself had not immediately reported the discussion. The delating fieldsman had come panting along with his news the moment he had been released from his match; I myself, being disengaged that afternoon, could have been hours before him. Since I had not been, the Father argued, I had clearly had no intention of reporting the matter at all, and now I must answer for this.

'But, before he proceeded against me for my laxity, he had to settle the far more important business of Greenacre's rebellion and proposed secession. Since the fieldsman who was listening to us had heard barely half of what was said, there were huge hiatuses. How and where had Greenacre procured the books that had corrupted him? What were they? What, exactly, was he proposing to do – always supposing that Father Jeremy would let him do anything? And so forth. Greenacre was obdurate. At the end of the term, he must have reasoned, he would just go home like anyone else, and with the help of his father he would be sent to a different and far preferable school. No one could stop this, provided he kept silence about it; but, if once they came to know what his plan was, there was no end to the trouble they could make between now and the end of the term, and even later. So he simply played the thing down by admitting that, yes, he had been reading works of dissidence, and, yes, he had found them interesting, and yes, he had told me something about them. But there was, he persisted, nothing more to it. It was a rather wicked game, and that was all. Let penance be done and life proceed. He was truly sorry to have caused worry.

'Father Jeremy, old hand as he was, knew that he was being flannelled. He discerned that what Greenacre wanted was delay.

Whatever else Greenacre's game was, it was clearly a waiting one. Time, then, was not on the good Father's side. Since Greenacre wouldn't answer his questions, then I must. There would be forgiveness of my crime, Father Jeremy proposed to me, if only I would tell him what he wanted to know. Details later: *what* was really behind all this? What was Greenacre *at*? Nothing, I said, taking the line agreed: Greenacre had got hold of these books, and he had found them interesting in a shocking sort of way, and . . .

'"Stop lying to me, boy," Father Jeremy said, "or you'll be in very bad trouble indeed."

'But I stood firm. As Greenacre pointed out, no one could prove anything more than the delating fieldsman had already divulged; nothing could prevail against silence.

'Father Jeremy never slackened in his efforts. He tried wooing, threatening, bribery, cursing, violence mimetic, metaphysical and mental; but Greenacre and I stuck to our story . . . until Father Jeremy sprang his master-stroke.

'He knew, because I had told him, that I was to spend the summer holidays with a favourite godfather in Scotland. Since my father was a soldier in Egypt and my mother had recently undergone a horrible operation, the aftermath of which would keep her in hospital for weeks and painfully convalescent for months, it had been decided to turn me over to "Uncle Balbo" in the Highlands, and since I loved both the man and the country I was yearning for the term to end and my visit to begin.

'Now, Giles, said Father Jeremy; you may not have realised this, but you have been placed, during this difficult period, in the care of a lawyer who has been instructed to work closely with us at Ampleforth. Hitherto we have consented to your spending the holidays with your godfather; but if we should have reason to think that you are in a harmful condition, spiritually or morally, then we shall recommend that you be sent on a prolonged retreat in some suitable religious house instead. If you persist in withholding the truth about your conversation with Greenacre, we shall conclude that you are indeed in a harmful condition, and we shall notify the lawyer and arrange for your retreat accordingly.

[109]

'This made me suddenly desperate. I had no doubt, you see, but that Father Jeremy and his colleagues had the power to do as he threatened. It did not occur to me to consult the lawyer, to urge that surely I could not be so brusquely disposable without regard to my own wishes. At fifteen you still believe what adults tell you, you know nothing of raising objections or appeals, you are terrified of "Making yourself a nasty little nuisance – and in war-time too!" I could not bear it. No Scotland with kind Uncle Balbo; instead the linoleum floors and plaster Madonnas and beastly chattering brothers in some suburban convent. I cracked, as Father Jeremy knew I would. I spilt wide open.

'Disaster,' said Giles, shivering lightly in the evening chill, 'followed for Greenacre. The monks instantly suborned his mother, who threatened a "nervous breakdown". How could she endure it, she said, if her only son broke with the Faith and was transferred to a school of infidels. She would sooner be dead. Greenacre's father, a man of good intentions, sound intelligence, and a character of straw, began to panic. Armed with his new money, he had been keen enough to get revenge on his wife, by arranging the apostasy of their son, for all the years of being dominated and taunted; but the prospect of hysterical disruption, to say nothing of being incessantly nagged at by unattractive monks about his duty to his "stricken" wife and "misguided" son, was too much for him. Shortly after I split, he caved in; and, as for the wretched Greenacre, he was sent into the retreat, which I had now escaped, in a Birmingham convent, there to repent his intellectual arrogance and his folly in challenging the earthly agents of God.

'When I told all this to Uncle Balbo a week or two later, he was exceedingly distressed. Why had I not consulted him? Well . . . there was no time, I hadn't thought of it, I was so sure Father Jeremy could do what he said . . . There had at least been time, said Uncle Balbo, to telephone him.

' "Telephone? But there isn't one there."

' "There is a public box just outside the grounds."

' "I hadn't any money, Uncle Balbo."

' "Nor the wit to reverse the charges?" '

' "What good would it have done?" '

' "I could have got hold of the lawyer, to make absolutely certain of my ground, and I could then have assured you that no matter what this bloody monk said you would still be coming to me for the summer holidays." '

' "You mean . . . Father Jeremy was lying?" '

' "I dare say he didn't know he was. He was carried away by what he conceived to be his mission, and he probably thought that his Head could at least put considerable pressure on the lawyer. But I'm afraid that one way or the other you were conned . . . so nastily conned that I am going to take it upon me to have *you* removed from Ampleforth. First I shall speak to the lawyer, then I shall be in touch, through the military authorities, with your father. Your mother need not, in her state of health, be consulted." '

'And so it was,' said Giles, as the moon peeped on to the veranda in Bangalore. 'The lawyers confirmed that no one from Ampleforth had even been in touch with them, and that they would absolutely not have permitted me to be incarcerated in a convent instead of visiting Uncle Balbo. They agreed that Father Jeremy's behaviour warranted my withdrawal from Ampleforth without notice. In fact they had been appointed *in loco parentis* to me for the duration of the war, so that they were free to act as they saw fit without further reference to anybody – though of course it was desirable that my father should be consulted should the exigencies of active service (secret service) in the South Egyptian deserts permit. Meanwhile, I must clearly be entered for a new school at Michaelmas. There were Catholic Schools of a less demanding nature than Ampleforth . . . or perhaps, in all the circumstances, a Church of England School might be considered.

' "What's your view?" said Uncle Balbo. "This is your big chance to break free from the Papists for good." '

' "I thought *you* were a Catholic, Uncle Balbo. Otherwise why are you my godfather?" '

' "Never mind what I am or might have been. You've seen how these brutes behave. Do you want to be done with them?" '

[111]

'I remembered Greenacre's remark about the "decency" of Church of England Schools and the "moderation" of the Church itself. But then look what had happened to Greenacre.

'"Your father and mother," Uncle Balbo was saying, "would not normally have allowed your removal, but they will not object very strongly when they find that it has actually happened and why. And again, these lawyers would not normally have agreed to such a course; you were placed in their care because two of the partners are Catholic; but the two Catholics are now away at the war, like your father, and their colleagues are liberal men who don't give a damn either way. So *now* you may escape if you wish. But at any moment the balance may alter. Your father could be posted home and be got at by these monks, or your mother may recover sufficiently to take an interest, or one of the lawyers may get cold feet at taking advantage of their partners' absence. So tell me *now*: do you, or do you not, wish to be placed in a non-Catholic school?"

'Remember Greenacre, I thought. Remember his song of "moderation" – and remember what had happened to the singer.

'"Yes, Uncle Balbo," I said; "but I should still like to go on being a Catholic."

'"Master Facing-Both-Ways. Luckily for you, that will be all right at the school I'm thinking of. You'll have to attend some ghastly red-brick horror with a bog priest inside it instead of the School Chapel, but that's up to you."'

So Giles had completed his education at a 'moderate' (in every sense) minor public school, out of reach of Father Jeremy's falsehoods and anathemas; his parents, when at length apprised of the change, simple accepted it as his Uncle Balbo (a very old friend) knew that they would (after all, Giles had not left the Roman Church); and everyone outside Ampleforth was happy.

'But what about those *inside* Ampleforth?' I said to Giles. 'What about Greenacre? How did he feel? His plans had been utterly buggered up by your treachery – as a result of which you escaped and he didn't.'

'He wrote me a very nice letter,' Giles said, 'saying it was a perfect example of *peripeteia*, of purpose effecting its own reversal. He said he quite understood why Father Jeremy's threat had been too much for me, and understood this even more clearly after three weeks in the Birmingham convent. As for his future, he had learned his lesson: *total* silence was the only solution, and next time he thought of a way out he wouldn't tell anybody at all. And after all, he added, he *had* to be free when he was over twenty-one . . . at which age he came into some money settled on him by his mother.'

'So that wasn't too bad,' I said.

'Unfortunately his mother heard about the way in which I had escaped from Ampleforth. She was so afraid lest some such lucky accident might set Greenacre free that she revoked the settlement and made Greenacre a conditional allowance instead. She wouldn't let him apply for entry to Oxford or Cambridge, she wouldn't even let him leave home once he'd left school. At first he didn't mind as he knew he'd get away when his time came for National Service – only it turned out that he had flat feet and was therefore exempt. He was absolutely trapped.'

'Couldn't his father – the one with the new money – do anything for him?'

'The father was so ashamed of the way he had already let Greenacre down that he turned into a drunk – he was well on the way already – and needs all his new money for himself. Greenacre is his mother's prisoner. If he tries to get any sort of job, she just writes to cancel it – says that he's delicate or not quite right in the head. She is going to possess him,' said Giles, 'and keep him in the Faith, until her dying day. And no doubt she'll think of some way of tying him up by mortmain. I delivered Greenacre to a vampire. And that is my reason,' said Giles, 'for resolving not to report you this time, or indeed any time, you or anybody else, ever again. I've seen what comes of reporting, of sneaking, as you call it. I have already done enough damage in that line, don't you think?'

'You also did *yourself* some good.'

'Did I? I thought I was going to be very happy when they sent me to Stowe. And at first I was. A pleasant, easy school, not too fierce about games or anything else; lovely architecture; tolerant yet adventurous schoolmasters, and friendly boys. You know what the trouble turned out to be?'

'I could try a guess. You got guilt about Greenacre?'

'Oh yes. But that would have happened wherever I went. There was something else . . . at Stowe.'

'Well?'

'Sex. The place was buzzing with it.'

'Most places are.'

'Not Ampleforth. Nor any of the Catholic schools. They really put a stopper on sex. So I wasn't used to it when I got to Stowe.'

'For Christ's sake! All you had to do was join in or keep out.'

'I couldn't keep out. A lot of people, attractive people, were keen on me, and I couldn't resist them. I'm strongly sexed, you see.'

'How very amusing for you.'

'But I *wanted* to keep out,' groaned Giles, under the Indian moon. 'I couldn't, but I wanted to. Because I knew it was *wrong*. Nobody else seemed to think it was. But I *knew*.'

'But how, for God's sake?'

'For God's sake, indeed. The monks had told me at Ampleforth.'

A T THE RISK of underlining what may already seem evident, I should like to make an observation or two on the fate of Roman Catholics (a) at Roman Catholic Public Schools, and (b) at Church of England Schools.

(a) It seems to me, from all that I have heard from Catholics and read of them, that the only two things which really matter at Catholic Schools are the Catholic Faith and Chastity. Since the

The School Hero

Cricket on the Head at Tonbridge

Football at Rugby

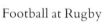

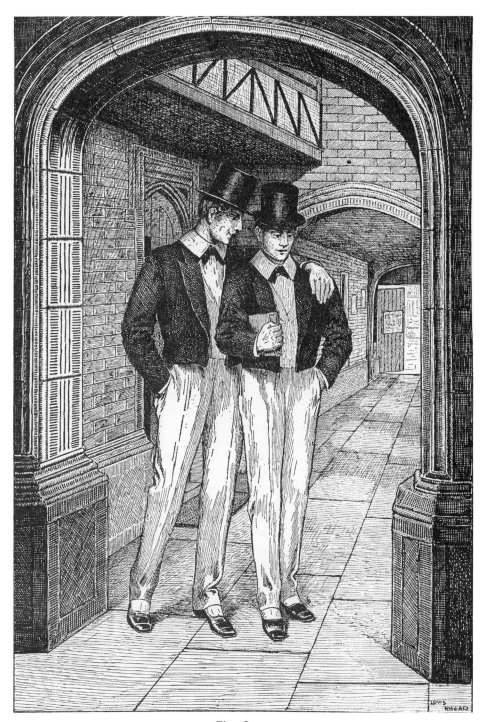

First Love

Classical and Modern: Charterhouse and Westminster

Cannon Fodder

The Field Marshal spotting military talent

'Alas, regardless of their doom, the little victims play!'

The Ring of Honour

masters are normally monks or priests of some kind, whose professional stock-in-trade is the former and who are dedicated for life to the latter, this is not surprising. And again, in the matter of Chastity we should remember that the Catholic Church holds sinful any sexual act (even within wedlock) which is not specifically directed towards propagation. Masturbatory or homosexual amusements, of however mild a kind, are therefore doubly damned: they are all, by definition, both extra-marital and sterile.

Now, strict inculcation of the Catholic Faith and the strict enforcement of Chastity (over what is only a tiny fraction of one's life) would not matter very much in themselves, were it not that the monks and priests involved remember from time to time that they are, after all, educating most of their boys for the World and that some attention must therefore be paid to worldly custom and practice. This consideration induces such teachers to acquire and disseminate a species of fake worldly knowledge and wisdom (fake, because entirely second-hand and theoretical, having no contact with experience) and to adopt certain fake worldly attitudes such as synthetic bonhomie or simulated tolerance. Unwary boys, deceived into accepting either the worldly wisdom or the worldly attitudes as genuine, will in the first place get a ludicrously perverted notion of the world and of the importance of the Catholics and their doctrine within it, and in the second will get some very nasty shocks if they put enough trust in their masters' 'tolerance' to try it to any extent beyond mere nursery peccadillo.

In case all this has not been sufficiently illustrated in Giles Freebody's tale, let me adduce one more very brief incidence of it. A Catholic friend of mine at Cambridge once told me that when he first arrived there he went at once (as bidden by his mentors at Downside) to wait upon the Roman Catholic Chaplain to the University. This elegant and apparently mundane paladin of the Church (the last priest whom ever I saw who affected frock coat with breeches and gaiters and a proper clerical top hat with 'flying buttresses') instructed my friend that it would be in his best interest to avoid certain series of lectures currently popular with intelligent men of all faculties and among them particularly Noël

Annan's course on the Nineteenth Century – 'brilliant, witty and stylish, as they tell me,' conceded the Chaplain, 'but deliberately provocative of doubt.'

When my chum disobeyed this injunction, he was immediately reported, by another Old Boy from Downside who had spotted him as he went in, to the Monsignor, who in his turn informed an important figure at Downside (perhaps even the Abbot himself) of this backsliding. A letter was sent to my friend which forbade him to visit old companions still at Downside until he had performed a painful and certified act of contrition.

(b) As for Catholics at Church of England Schools, they were regarded, in my day, as mildly repulsive oddities, who were compelled to attend some hideous Catholic shack in a bungaloid suburb, where they were harangued by unshaven Irish priests of the lowest class out. Some of these unhappy boys tried to proselytise, with indifferent success, others had the good sense to hold their tongues on the subject of religion.

Nobody knowingly tried to seduce a Roman Catholic, for fear of 'priest trouble', and the laxer and more lascivious RCs strongly resented this. Many of these Laodiceans, appreciating the charm of the C of E liturgy (I am, of course, referring to the liturgy used forty years ago and not to the muck that has been foisted upon us since) and deploring the gabbled Latin of some jumped-up potato peasant in a cassock, quietly transferred their patronage to the School Chapel and often apostasised altogether. Even then they were still regarded as unsafe by amorists, *pace* the sexual popularity enjoyed by Giles Freebody at his second school.

H AVING BEEN COMMISSIONED AT BANGA-LORE, 200 Second Lieutenants of Infantry, we were all found to be surplus to any possible requirement in the Far East and were sent back to England, where nobody wanted us either. So we were seconded to units of the Artillery, the Engineers, etc, etc, where we made incompetent nuisances of ourselves for the next year or so until we were duly 'demobbed'. Forgiven my scandal at Charterhouse on the strength of my exemplary military career, I proceeded to King's College, Cambridge, where I took up residence at the beginning of the Long Vacation Term, 1948, in order to recover regular and scholarly habits against the start of the Academic Year in October.

When I first arrived in Cambridge, I still had no doubt of the excellence of the public school system and the efficacy (*ceteris paribus*) of its products. I associated it with a commission for me, a scholarship at King's for me, comfort and consideration for me, people calling me 'sir' and deferentially doing what I told them: all very proper. For the rest, it seemed to me that most public school boys were pretty easy to get on with, no matter how disagreeable they were at bottom, because they were all conversant with a code of manners that forbade awkward questions, was rich in soothing euphemisms and neat formulae for evading crucial issues, and ensured that in no case whatever should public school men break ranks if threatened or attacked by aliens or renegades (for deserters we certainly had) – by socialists, intellectuals or just plain yobs in the street.

The three paramount qualities of a public school boy, it seemed to me, were loyalty, moderation and fair-mindedness, all of which qualities might be subsumed, for all practical purposes, under the one term, 'decency', and what could be better than that? Of course public schoolboys included bilkers, bullies, shits, tyrants, black-mailers and thieves; but these somehow took on much of the charm and seemliness of the surroundings in which they had been educated, so that public school thieves were turned out in the mould of Raffles, for example, bilkers or blackmailers in that of Rawdon Crawley or Burgo Fitzgerald.

Although I had heard a lot of criticism of the public schools, from the blind hatred of the boot-black at Cordwalles to the guilty moral distaste of Giles Freebody, it seemed to me that those that took exception were on the whole the exceptions, and that the causes of their hostility were either ignorance, envy, prudery, priggery or spite. It had not yet occurred to me that those outside the charmed circle might feel resentment or even fury at having fair opportunity denied them or their proven talents disregarded. It had not come within my notice that what we, as public school or ex-public school men, found moving or amusing, was often to others false, irrelevant or cruel.

But from 1948 on I began to understand that such good qualities as loyalty or steadfastness (properties by no means peculiar to public school men alone) did not altogether justify snobbery or abuse of privilege, and that rather too many working class gladiators were butchered to make upper class holidays. Yet despite this creeping doubt I continued to admire – to love – the best of the public school type and to tolerate and smile at the defects and antics of the worst. The public schools produce men in whose company I am at ease, for better or for worse, and who provide spectacles and entertainments of which I seldom tire. Conscious of the faults and the inequities, I recognise the achievements: gratified by the achievements, I condone the inequities and the faults. This is the easier as I find, despite all moral injunction to the contrary, that the inequities (and even the iniquities) are ironic judgments on the bovine inertia of the rest of the human race, which is too lazy and futile to remedy the matter; and that the faults are slily appropriate to the merits. Thus to lead men you must be a convincing liar, and to rescue women you must handle their most intimate parts.

And so, as I shall hope to show in the pages that follow, the more critical I became of the public schools, and the more clearly I recognised their vices and the strength of the arguments against them, the more enjoyable and in many ways the more admirable I found them. My fondness for the public schools is rather like that of the Athenians for Alcibiades: 'the more they disapproved of him, the more they hungered for him.'

One of my greatest friends at King's was a boy called Francis (now Professor) Sherlock. Francis had been a Colleger (Scholar or

'Tug') at Eton, of which he spoke with some repugnance, assigning as his reason for this his distaste for 'games' and 'heartiness'. On one occasion, when I asked him to be more precise – how far was *he* made to take part in games or to cheer on the touchline (etc, etc)? – he remarked that it was not so much what he was made to *do* that he resented as what he was expected to *feel*.

'We had all won our places in College by the use of our brains or intellects,' he said, 'and in typical human fashion we set ourselves to biting the hands – or rather the heads (our own) – that fed us. We openly and constantly repudiated the exercise of the mind, skimped and scamped our school work, blackguarded literature and the arts. In order to show that we were not just nasty little swots, we – or most of us – tried to be more aggressively philistine, more exclusively athletic and physical, than any other group of boys in the entire school . . . and so, by extension, more 'manly', more conventional (i.e. anti-Bohemian), more military (this was during the war, of course, when the Corps loomed very large), and more morally correct – in all things, as you might say, more straight-faced and more straight-backed.

'Look around at the Old Etonians in this College. The Oppidans are for the most part genial, civil and tolerant men who take people very much as they find them. But the ex-Collegers, the one-time scholars of the foundation, are for ever rushing down to the river with ostentatious whoops, or accusing people of being "queer", or jostling "the aesthetes" on their way into chapel. You will have heard, I dare say, of this horrid business about Henry?'

And indeed I had. Henry, like Francis, had been a 'Tug' at Eton, and like Francis very much disposed to mock and satirise the Philistinism and heartiness of the other Collegers, who had lost no opportunity of persecuting them both in return. Since then Francis and Henry had given fresh cause for irritation. For, while both of them had been clever enough to win open scholarships to King's, many of their contemporaries had only managed to obtain scholarships or exhibitions which were 'tied' or limited to Old Etonians, and thus of distinctly inferior academic value – and for the most part worth much less in cash. Both disparities rankled; oddly enough, though most Collegers affected to despise intellectual matters, they were not at all pleased at being beaten by Francis and Henry in intellectual competition . . . leave aside the monetary differential.

There were also complications about Class. What had been seen in a glass darkly at Eton was made very plain at King's: not only were Collegers inferior to Oppidans in social rank (that much had been crystal clear while they were still at Eton) but they also lacked poise, cachet and style. The post-National Service Oppidans with their Guards or Cavalry blazers, their liberal allowances, their knowledge of food and drink, and their civilised manners, made the post-National Service Tugs, with their Fusilier or Light Infantry blazers, their tenuous resources and their habitual want of *savoir-vivre* or *savoir-faire*, look like a herd of ill-conditioned donkeys that had strayed into a stud farm.

So the Collegers, riled by recognition of their own dowdiness, if compared with the Oppidans, and of their own dimness, if compared with their fellow Collegers Francis and Henry, needed someone on whom to take out their resentment. The well-bred Oppidans they would not dare to attack or annoy; on the contrary, they cringed and snivelled before them. But Francis and Henry, whose attitudes had always been provocative . . . Francis and Henry, who had presumed to hog superior scholarships . . . Francis and Henry, who were preening themselves because no one, now, could invoke the Spartan regulations of College to cut them down to size or to punish their pretensions . . . Francis and Henry would do very well for a bit of a biff.

But Francis, they found, must be exempt from conspicuous insult or injury because he was a Jew and they could not now afford (whatever might have been the case at Eton) to appear before the world, in the climate of 1948, as anti-Semitic. This left them with Henry: Henry and his delicately furnished rooms, Henry and his painting by – who was the bloody man? – Jacques-Émile Blanche, Henry and his Beardsley drawings of Venus and Cupid, his vile and scandalous delight.

The campaign against Henry began with a deputation. Three Old Collegers went to Henry in his room and pointed out, coolly but politely, that Henry's airs, furnishings and general accoutrement were 'giving College a bad name in King's'. His decoration, they said, perverse in taste; his picture by Jacques-Émile Blanche was a portrait of the flaunting arch-decadent, Jean Cocteau; and his Beardsley drawings, of Venus pleasuring her son, were unspeakably disgusting.

How did they know, enquired Henry, that his Beardsley drawings were of Venus pleasuring her son?

Informed rumour, they said; no smoke, etc.

'Would you like to have a look at them? So that you can be sure?'

'??!! . . . Er . . . Well . . . Yes.'

So the famous drawings were produced and turned out to be, not indeed of Venus pleasuring her son, but of her son pleasuring Venus.

A dainty and newly pubescent Cupid began by powdering his mother's bottom while she stroked herself, then came round in front, between her splayed knees, and paid her an intimate oral compliment (one of the few extant examples of Beardsley's treatment of this practice), then mounted and penetrated her, found her two spacious to retain his piping (impressive as this now was for one of his age), finally went behind her and entered her by the postern, while a poodle lapped at her parted labia.

Stupefied and tumescent the deputation departed.

The next day it was back.

'Come for another squint?' Henry said.

'How dare you . . how dare you try to involve us in an orgy? You hoped to get us into a funny mood, and then –'

'– Nothing of the kind. I'm as normal as you are,' said Henry, quite truthfully.

'Well then. Admit that you keep those pictures to – er – rouse people.'

'The only people that I want to – er – rouse, are girls; and girls do not get – er – roused by rude pictures.'

'Oh,' said the deputation, which was learning something.

'But,' said Henry, 'I sometimes find . . . that if there are no girls around . . . it is fun to – er – rouse myself.'

'How foul,' said the deputation.

'Very agreeable,' said Henry: 'and don't start telling me my eyes are going to fall out.'

An Oppidan called Adrian Kurtz came in, wearing a Guards tie.

'Henry darling,' he fluted, 'can I look at your delicious piccies? I do so love that little Cupid and his scrummy member. You won't mind if I have it off while I'm looking?'

'Not in the least,' said Henry.

'Now we have seen and heard enough,' said the deputation, and filed out.

The end of the story had been something of an anti-climax. No wrecking of Henry's room, no debagging of Henry or chucking him into his namesake the VI's fountain, no Savonarolan bonfires: simply a self-righteous protest, alleging obscenity and corruption, to the Tutor . . . who would dearly have liked to have ignored it but knew that if he did so he in turn would be reported to the Provost of King's or the Headmaster of Eton for condoning flagrant immorality. As it was, he showed considerable courage by insisting, to the Provost and Council, that Henry should only be rusticated, not sent down for good and all.

'Even so,' said Francis to me, 'a very dismal story.'

'Eton, whether College or the rest of it, is outside my range,' I said; 'but I do think Adrian Kurtz might have been a little less flamboyant.'

'Adrian is a relatively recent convert to pederasty,' said Francis, 'and so all the more enthusiastic and demonstrative.'

'Not very sensible. Come to think of it, I've seen him in chapel, not a million miles from the Choir Stalls.'

'You'll find that Adrian will never go too far. That's one of the things that Eton specialises in teaching Oppidans – a preparation for the public life which so many of them will lead.'

'But surely – he's already gone too far. In Henry's room, in front of that ghastly deputation.'

'No. If he had, he'd have been rusticated like Henry. All he did, he could plausibly claim, was to ask to see those pictures, and make a silly joke. No one actually saw him "have it off" – even if he did.'

'But, if he hadn't behaved like that, those Collegers of yours would never have reported Henry.'

'Oh yes they would. Middle class spite. The point was, you see, that Henry, who is one of them, had somehow promoted himself to Oppidan status – he was the chap that owned the drawings that brought the rich and noble ex-Ensign of the Grenadier Guards hot foot to Henry's room, where he addressed him as "darling". They resented Kurtz, of course, but it's what they expected of him and so they could bear it. But *Henry's part* in the whole thing they found quite intolerable. Henry should have been licking Kurtz's suede boots, not being treated on terms of intimacy. And so it was Henry they went for.'

'Did I understand you to say that Kurtz is "noble"?'

'Almanach de Gotha.'

'And what was all that about his being a recent convert to pederasty? One would have thought he started at his prep. school, the way he carries on.'

'Oh no. Kurtz,' said Francis, 'was the spottiest, weediest, spindliest, stupidest boy in my year at Eton. God knows why he'd been accepted by R—, the most fashionable Tutor. Something to do with having had his name put down very early, I suppose. Adrian Kurtz was, quite literally, beneath contempt. People couldn't even be bothered to despise him. He simply didn't exist. As for his family, it was a joke: minor Belgian barons who owned a button factory. Since his parents were dead, he lived, during the holidays, with a guardian uncle in Cheltenham, who was so ashamed of him that he shut him away in a bedroom and a few feet of garden. So Kurtz grew up knowing nothing of anything, in complete obscurity both at school and at what he called home.

'Then suddenly a lot of things happened to him. First, he lost his spots. Then he turned out to be quite presentable and also to be a pretty fair historian, albeit with a Catholic bias (he'd had the run of his uncle's library to keep him happy). He was promoted up the school, became a member of Library in his Tutor's, and chose a scrumptious, but scrumptious, study fag. *Chose him in all inno-cence*. He simply had not realised that "that kind of thing" existed. He *still* didn't realise. He hadn't even masturbated, he told me the other day, and thought that wet dreams gave you a nice feeling because they were caused by the retention of urine which some-how began to tickle your parts. He chose the boy because the boy, wanting a privileged appointment, smiled slily at him. Kurtz thought that this was an expression of good will – nothing more – and took him on . . . and was then amazed by the number of people, distinguished people, that suddenly wanted to know Kurtz himself.

' "Don't bother about it just now," the Captain of Boats would say, *à propos* of nothing at all; "send your boy round with a note."

' "Let me know when you can manage tea," a member of Pop would remark, "no, not now, no hurry – send your fag round with a list of dates."

'In no time, Kurtz was one of the most sought-after men in the school. He was given some kind of cap for Fives and then another for Cricket and he was eventually elected to Pop, simply in order that he might send his etherially beautiful fag on messages to the mighty. And still he himself remained innocent. Then one day, after he had left and was training with the Brigade Squad at Pirbright – he had been promoted high in the Corps so that the big brass could ask for frequent reports to be delivered to them by his study fag, and in the end was recommended for a commission in the Grenadiers – one day he suddenly realised something very peculiar. All those grand people with whom he had exchanged messages at Eton – somehow it had always been arranged that *he* should send his boy to *them* rather than the other way round. "Take your time and then send your boy" – that had been the formula. So he went to an Etonian friend in the Brigade Squad – one who had constantly been asking him to "send his boy" – asked him the relevant question and received the relevant answer. Whereupon, in a revelation as sudden if not as edifying as that of Saul at Tarsus, he saw what he had been missing. He went down to Eton that very week-end, and there visited, dazzled and seduced a

[124]

fourteen-year-old especially recommended by his chum in the Brigade Squad. Since then he has never looked back.'

'Then he'd better look *out*, or he may find himself in prison.'

'I doubt it. I told you, Oppidans are trained never to go too far . . . which means, in practice, never to commit themselves until the other fellow is committed first. There used to be a special Oppidan technique of seduction which ensured that you had a water-tight and highly respectable excuse in case of complaint or detection at any stage of the proceedings. Thus,

'"Don't make a silly fuss, Nugent. I was only practising the fireman's lift on you. We've got a test in it in Corps this afternoon." "Oh well, if that's all you were doing, Buffington Tumper, of course I don't mind at all. Perhaps you'd like to practise some more?" Or,

'"I say, sir, what a jolly good thing you came along so un-expectedly. Weyland-Neddler's got a beastly mosquito bite on his groin, and we were just wondering whether he ought to go to m'Dame. Perhaps you'd better take a look first – we mustn't waste her time when there's a war on." Or, in extreme cases,

'"He didn't know what was the matter, sir, when it suddenly went like that. He thought he was ill. But as soon as he showed me I was able to explain. Why am I in the same condition, sir? Because I had to show him it was quite normal and happened to every-body."'

There was even, as Francis went on to explain, a convention that however suspicious the interloper might be, he must accept these excuses, provided they were framed in the prescribed and traditional form, on the ground that they were profferred 'on the word of one gentleman to another'.

I T WAS SURPRISING, I found as I grew older, how many elements in school life declared themselves or became comprehensible only long after one had left. Before one went, one was too green to understand and the prospect was too close: while one was there one was too buffeted about by day-to-day necessity to observe and analyse accurately: but, after one had left, one could look back calmly, seek rational explanation from the right sources, and carefully collate all the answers.

As I have indicated, by the time I arrived in Cambridge I was beginning to realise that there were far more snakes and far more different kinds of injurious fruit inside the public schoool Eden than I had any reason to suppose while I was inside it or had just left it myself. Even the invidious manner of my going had only served to make more desirable the people and the way of life that I had left. But now that I had been a good while outside the garden, I recognised, in their true shape, all sorts of deleterious and unwholesome creatures that had been forcibly expelled by the Angel, or had crawled out under the wall, or had sidled out shiftily through the gate. Most of these had seemed all right inside the garden: it was only now that they had left it that they appeared misshapen or diseased.

An interesting example of this phenomenon comes to mind from my days with the Shropshire Light Infantry, which I joined as a Regular after leaving Cambridge, having failed to find employment elsewhere. It concerns three people who, inside the garden (in this case Shrewsbury School), had filled the more or less harmless traditional roles of School Hero, School Martinet and School Busybody, and had indeed continued in much the same characters (*mutatis mutandis*) for many years after entering the Army . . . until in early middle age they suddenly suffered hideous transformations as a result of differences that could never have arisen and motives that could never have operated had not all three been contemporaries at the same public school.

Shortly after I had joined my battalion in Germany, we heard that a certain James Bartrum was to come to us in a few weeks' time as our new Second-in-Command. Bartrum, though now only a

Major, had been a temporary Brigadier during the war and had for a short time commanded an entire Division (during the illness of the GOC) with accuracy and verve. This success had made him many enemies among less talented and glittering regulars, and steps had been taken, after the war, to strap him tightly down in his substantive rank.

It was Bartrum, needless to say, charming, handsome, versatile, witty, easy-going, open-handed, easy-coming, who had been the School Hero in his day at Shrewsbury (210 not out against the Gentlemen of Shropshire and two hat tricks in the same innings against the MCC).

One of those who had most resented Bartrum's war-time glory was Lieutenant-Colonel Sextus Whyte, at present Commanding Officer of our Battalion. Dark and gristly, Whyte had been in the same house as Bartrum at Shrewsbury, where he had been a very decent long distance runner but was altogether overshadowed by Bartrum, the golden cricketer. He had also been a conscientious Head of House, just and impartial, much concerned with propriety and regulation, loathed by almost all, who (of course) adored Bartrum the Athenian, his next in order.

Whyte was even more unpopular than he need have been because he employed as jackal a runty boy called Popham, who lurked about the place sniffing out delinquency, then went groising off to sneak to Whyte. Nobody would much have minded this (there is a professional goody-goody in every house at every school) had not Whyte and Popham between them squeezed a cruel ichor of blame and punishment from occurrences so petty as to be, on any normal reckoning, negligible. A failure to hang one's coat straight, a slightly clumsy knot in one's tie, an unthinking use of the word 'blast' – trivialities such as these were paid for with sweat and toil beyond any equitable ratio.

I should add, at this point that Popham was now the senior company commander in our battalion in Germany.

So now: consider first the position at Shrewsbury some twenty years before: shrewish Whyte in titular command of the House; blazing Bartrum as his immediate (officially loyal but in truth contemptuous) lieutenant; and sneaky Popham, the informer, who longed, above all things, to catch Bartrum out in overt treachery to Whyte. This would have been a normal enough set of people and circumstances in any school whatever, and more or less harmless, because in the school were adult masters, as in the Garden of Eden there had been Angels, to guide the boys and see that no harm was done. Only after the devil had worked his work, and Adam and Eve were *outside* the garden and beyond the guidance of the Angels within, could they do real damage in human terms; and so with Whyte, Bartrum and Popham – only after time had worked his work and they were outside Shrewsbury School would their full potentiality for evil be realised. It would not *necessarily* be realised even then, and indeed during the years that had passed since they left Shrewsbury all three had had quite useful careers, in Bartrum's case an occasionally brilliant one. But now they were about to be together again in the same grouping as at Shrewsbury: Whyte, the CO, a lean, mean, ascetic man who soldiered by the book; Bartrum, the bold and beautiful Sir Lancelot, as his Second-in-Command; and Popham the messenger to pry and delate. The same grouping as at Shrewsbury, but with one difference: this time, in the King's Shropshire Light Infantry, there were no masters to dispel their intrigues with a snap of the fingers or douse their quarrels with a handful of dust; *they* were their own masters now.

At Shrewsbury Whyte, who was a term senior to Bartrum and had left a term before him, had done his bitter best to prevent Bartrum from succeeding him as Head of House. He had urged on the house-master that Bartrum was frivolous, fickle and quite possibly amorous; that his grace and facility lent him an ease that was bad for his own moral character and a perilous example to others; that he was a polluted vessel from which none should be allowed to drink. All to no avail; the house-master, a cricketer like Bartrum, liked the boy, admired the player, recognised the natural leader – and made no bones about it to Whyte.

'You,' he said, 'are a diligent, pedantic, reliable Head of the House. With you here, I know that everything will be *en règle* from one end of the term to the other. I also know that there will be no proper spirit in the House. Respect perhaps, fear certainly, but no love and no delight. I am grateful for your hard work and efficiency. The fact remains that you are like a cold, grey day with low, dank cloud. With Bartrum we shall have the sun again – we shall have Apollo.'

So despite Whyte's moral protest and Popham's assiduous sniffing for dirt Bartrum came to the throne when Whyte departed, louring and unlamented, for Sandhurst, and Popham crept away, taking no farewell for none would bid him it, to a crammer in Ealing.

And now was their chance for a re-play. Soon after Bartrum's posting had been announced to us, it was plausibly rumoured and then unofficially confirmed that, all things being strictly equal, Bartrum was to succeed Whyte as Commanding Officer. He had done long enough penance for his war-time success (we heard) and most of his enemies were gone. But not Whyte and Popham. Defeated, *humiliated* twenty years ago in their efforts to keep Bartrum from being Head of House, they now had a superb opportunity to get their revenge in kind. If they could keep Bartrum out of the Command of the Battalion, they would have won back ten times over what they lost when he inherited the House.

Bartrum arrived; Whyte bristled; Popham lurked. Whyte's tactical aim was to net a bag of oral indiscretions and minor derelictions, for which the fluent and easy-going Bartrum was well known, and to present these to higher authority, e.g. the Colonel of the Regiment, as indications of light-mindedness and of unsuitability for Command. But Whyte and Popham were out of luck. Warned by past experience of this pair and also by his well-wishers, who had been studying the form for months, Bartrum was scrupulous in keeping his mouth shut and his nose clean. This was his chance – his last chance – to resuscitate his career, and he was determined to take it: not a joke, not a gesture should escape him that might be cast up to his discredit. The effect of all this was to turn him into another and altogether less amiable –

in fact downright disagreeable – person. Instead of the jolly, friendly, generous, civilised and adventurous man whom his friends had told us all to expect, we found a morose, taut, suspicious, snapping and nagging scold, who hardly dare let fall a civil word lest he be accused of favouritism, who hardly dare drink a small glass of sherry lest he be dubbed a drunk.

As for Whyte and Popham, they too were transformed. From being two dull and unpopular but in the main tolerable officers, they became, from the day of Bartrum's arrival, a pair of scheming fiends, and then, when they realised that Bartrum was now a model of impregnable virtue, a pair of disappointed and thwarted fiends. Imagine the reaction of Milton's Satan if Adam and Eve had refused the apple. The creeping serpent would have become an encased vortex of hissing and writhing frustration. So it was here, and so it continued for some weeks: Whyte simmered and fumed, phosphorescent with venom; Popham prowled like a seething vampire; while Bartrum, the hunter turned squatter, the hitter turned blocker, played a dead bat and persisted in a static condition of grace.

It then occurred to Whyte that the way to provoke a man to folly or misdemeanour was not to treat him as an enemy but to hail him as a friend – to encourage him to relax, flatter him a little, tell him that everything is now all right. He therefore sent for Bartrum one morning, apologised for the frigidity of his bearing over the last few weeks, and explained that he had been conducting a test of Bartrum's fitness for command. Nothing, elaborated Whyte, was a better measure of a man's character than his behaviour when treated with hostility and disdain. If his confidence and capacity could survive that, they could survive anything. Clearly, this was the case with Bartrum; he had passed the ordeal with flying colours; Whyte would now notify the Colonel of the Regiment that he totally endorsed Bartrum's appointment as the next CO.

Bartrum, easy, genial Bartrum, tired and disgusted by his pose as puritan, welcomed the words of benevolent truce. Forgetting the intrigues at Shrewsbury many years before, forgetting the wiles exercised to oust him there and the snarling fury which attended their failure, he believed what he had been told, took three glasses of wine at luncheon, made two clever and injurious jokes about the local GOC which had the table in fits, and then went out to take his part in Umpiring the Battalion Sports.

Whyte, both as Athlete and CO, set great store by these. Of all the events his favourite was the one in which he himself had been distinguished, the Cross Country Race. This he followed closely, patrolling the course in his jeep as *aficionado* and also Chief Umpire, following the leading group then doubling back to check on the loiterers, racing forward to the leaders again, overseeing all things meticulously from the start outside the Guard Room, up through the meadows and into the pine forest, along the ridge, down through the orchards and round the lake, back up the hill and into the barracks . . . where the contestants were required to run three times round the quarter-mile running track to make up a full five miles. In charge on the running track was James Bartrum, whose job it was to see that the runners did their fair three laps and to warn them, by ringing a hand-bell, when the leader had completed the first two and begun the last.

As Bartrum and his group of assistants waited on the track for the long-distance runners to traverse field and forest and return to barracks, he chatted easily of this and that, talked of good times past and the better yet to come, chaffed old comrades, took out and re-touched the old jokes, welcomed new voices and new faces. So that when the runners appeared nobody really noticed them. All hung wholly on James Bartrum's words (except the beady Popham) and James, released into loquacity after long weeks of sullen silence, revelled in his performance and his audience. He was still revelling during the first lap and the second; but, as the leader was near completing the third and last, he looked up, recalled his duties, and thinking this must still be the *penultimate* lap, rang his bell. With despair the runners staggered past the post and started on a fourth and supererogatory circuit. There were those that would have stopped, had not an officious Company

Sergeant-Major, thinking he was saving the occasion, called out . . .

'Come on, come on, no skiving. You heard the officer ring the bell and you know what *that* means: last lap *now*, whatever you thought before'

. . . and thus underlined and italicised (so to speak) the hideous error of Major James Bartrum.

Whyte dismounted from his jeep; he paused to speak with Popham, who had moved towards him from his place on the fringes of the group round Bartrum; he nodded, then gestured to Popham to follow him.

As Whyte approached Bartrum's group, its members, mostly NCOs and junior officers, drew back to make a passage for him, so that he might come at Major Bartrum, who stood with his face crumpled and his whole body sagging, as Oscar Wilde must have stood when he made his fatal *bêtise* in the witness box ('Did you ever kiss him, Mr Wilde?' 'Oh dear me no, he was much too plain'), still dangling his silly bell.

'An unfortunate mistake, James,' said Whyte: 'those poor devils have already run five miles. It doesn't really look very good, now does it? A lucky thing the Colonel of the Regiment isn't here . . . though of course he will have to hear about it. Perhaps you would like to ask two of these gentlemen to accompany you to your quarters, where they can look after you . . . until you are yourself.'

Our next Commanding Officer was Lieutenant-Colonel Popham.

W HEN I LEFT THE ARMY for the second time, having resigned my commission after backing too many slow horses, I became a writer of essays and reviews, then a writer of novels, and then, a little later, a writer of radio and screen plays.

Much of what I wrote was about the Public Schools, as this was one of the subjects which I was supposed to understand.

One day a prep. school master invited me to come and watch a football match at his school, and as we stood on the touch line he said:

'Why is it that your stuff on the public schools is only about the worst side of them?'

'I write as I find.'

'Then you find a lot of filth.'

Perhaps. But the grubs that feed on filth, they say, turn into painted butterflies. The fact that there is a great deal wrong with public schools, a great deal that is unjust, disgusting, cruel and filthy, does not seem to me to detract from their charm, and certainly not from the charm and peculiarities of those that have attended them.

'*Sum*,' I am: I am who I am: perhaps that was what we meant when we answered our names on the roll at Charterhouse, that we were confident in ourselves and our own personalities, and were very far from being the ground-down, rigidly conventional and conforming wretches whom one legend about the public schools would have us be. On the contrary: as I have tried to show here, public school boys are splendid in their resource, their eccentricities, their wilfulness, their determination to have their own way, in the honour and loyalty which they display despite their incessant self-seeking, in their overall kindness to their own kind and in the occasional and inexorable sentences of death or exile which they pass on that kind, above all in their will to survive, and on their own terms at that. Survival, after all, is the name of the world's game; and it is still played most brilliantly and stylishly (so I believe) by men that have been to a public school.

Sum: I am who I am. But we must not forget *Adsum*: I am here. I am here, I am a part of all this, I am *of* this world of which I have written here, I know it, I admire it, I cherish it, I love it. I wish it well, now and for ever. And for those who hate it or wish to destroy it (and they are many), the socialists and the crabs and the spoil-sports and the do-gooders and the square-toes and the prudes and the prigs and the egalitarians with their sanctimonious and drivelling cant – for them I wish drowning in a midden and a pauper's funeral on a wet Monday in Brixton or Toxteth.

Index